Affair of CONVENIENCE

JENNIFER AUGUST

AFFAIR OF CONVENIENCE

Cover Design and Interior Format by
The Killion Group
www.thekilliongroupinc.com

Dedication

For Susan Gable who believed in this book from the very beginning. A special thank you to Sherri Nelson Vest for her invaluable insights into all things opera.

Chapter One

"Let me make love to you."

Taryn Kirkpatrick's eyes slit open at the husky, sensual male voice echoing in her head. Groggily she reached out. Her hand swept over the cool cotton sheet on the bed next to her. Empty.

With a half-smile and a sigh, she closed her eyes, snuggling into the blankets. A pleading litany for his return tumbled through her mind as she drifted back to sleep.

His hands were warm, strong, demanding. No part of her skin escaped his touch. His palm slid down her throat, over her breasts, slipping between her parted legs.

"Mmm." She tilted her hips.

"You like that?"

Eyes closed in concentration, she nodded, unable to put into words the aching need he was rousing in her. She didn't want to talk, only feel. He was incredible. The best lover she'd ever had.

And she didn't even know his name.

"Who are you?" she whispered, forcing her

eyes open.

He lifted his dark head from her stomach and smiled. The corners of his green eyes crinkled with the movement. Two long dimples flashed in his cheeks.

"Who do you want me to be?" He kissed her abdomen and her muscles contracted.

Taryn's lids fluttered shut again and she palmed one of his muscular shoulders.

"Taryn?" His sure hands touched her everywhere she longed to be touched, stroked her to absolute distraction.

"Just you," she managed, tugging at him. "Kiss me."

He slid up her body, one hand still cupping her, his thumb rubbing a devilish rhythm against her clit. He levered up on his elbow, staring down at her, the smile still on his face.

Taryn licked her lips. She knew exactly how his mouth felt on hers. Knew the exquisite taste and wetness of his tongue. She lifted her head.

He met her halfway, kissing her softly, lightly, then moved away. She followed him while thrusting her hips against his hand.

"Please," she whispered, wrapping her fingers around his wrist.

He opened his mouth but only a low buzz emerged. He frowned slightly, then grinned and kissed her again, a hard, fast kiss that left her more breathless than before. He shifted his hand, circling her clit with more urgency.

Taryn gasped and slammed her eyes shut, legs wide and taut in anticipation. She clenched her butt and held her breath.

So close.

The buzz sounded again and she shook her head, fighting to hold on to the building orgasm. A few more strokes and—

The loud piercing screech of her alarm clock shattered the moment, jerking Taryn from the edge of orgasm to cold-shower deflation in seconds.

"No," she muttered, smacking at the clock before burrowing her face into the pillow. "Come back," she pleaded.

A few more minutes of desperately trying to return to sleep proved fruitless. Her dream lover wasn't coming back today. And she wasn't coming, period.

She groaned and stretched, cursing alarm clocks, the need for a day job and the guy at the coffee shop who'd started this madness.

"Meow."

A not-so-light weight settled in the small of her back.

"I'm up, Velvet."

Soft paws kneaded her backside, and the cat's tail whapped gently against her spine. "Meow," the cat said with more force.

"I can't get up until you get off of me."

With one last long stretch, Velvet jumped down.

Taryn rolled over, uncomfortably aware of the sensual tension still running through her. Her panties slid against her crotch, touching off another round of sensation.

Taryn debated finishing herself, but one look at her furry, ebony cat and she decided not to.

"It wouldn't be the same anyway."

Velvet's round golden eyes stared back silently before she turned on her paws and minced out of the room and down the hall.

Taryn sat up, reaching for her chenille robe and shrugging into it. She yawned as she trudged through the hallway. She needed something to calm her down. Coffee. She stumbled into the door leading to the kitchen.

Coffee Guy's face immediately popped into her mind, totally distracting her.

It was the same face from her dreams. The same face that had kept her hot, bothered and unsatisfied for the past three weeks.

Ever since the day she'd run into him at Cuppa Joe's, he'd plagued her dreams with wild imaginings of wet kisses and hot sex.

And she didn't even know his name. Had never even had a conversation with him. But she knew his voice was as smooth and rich as the black coffee he drank and his butt as tight and perfect as the cinnamon rolls she bought. She spent enough time in line behind him ogling his buns, she ought to know.

"ME-OW."

"Okay, okay," she muttered, scooping out some crunchy fish-flavored food for the cat.

"I am not going today. Absolutely not. Who needs cinnamon rolls three times in one week?"

Velvet ignored her completely as she daintily ate her kibbles.

Taryn returned to her room, doffed her robe and nightgown and pulled on a pair of black jeans. Opening her dresser drawer, she surveyed the assortment of bras, before deciding on a wild leopard print that pushed her breasts up and out. Now she needed a shirt that would show them off to their best advantage. Just in case he showed up.

Taryn growled in disgust at herself, even as she pulled a royal blue, scoop neck t-shirt from her closet. She was going to Joe's.

Cooper Malone picked up the phone and called his secretary. "Ginger, I need—"

"Hang on, boss."

"Ginger," he gritted out. "Bring me the—"

"Just one sec, I promise." The receiver clattered against her desk, and Coop cursed as he jerked his head away, ear ringing as he reminded himself why he kept her. She knew the filing system, she could read his writing, she was his best friend's little sister, she bought his dates great flowers.

"Sorry 'bout that," Ginger said, a breathless grin in her voice. "What do you need?"

"A secretary who knows who's boss. Failing that, I'll take the Gleason file." Coop shoved the receiver back onto its cradle and rubbed a hand over his mouth. This day had to be absolutely perfect. Nothing could go wrong.

He'd even skipped going to Joe's for his morning coffee. Not only did he not need a caffeine high, but he didn't need the distraction of the woman with ice-blue eyes and low-cut shirts. She had a pair of perfectly round, luscious-looking breasts that kicked him into gear better than coffee. He'd only seen her a few times, but she was not the kind of woman a man easily overlooked.

He bet she'd be great in bed. A body made for sin and lips made for wrapping around—

His door swung open and Ginger sped inside, a manila folder under her arm, a thermo-carafe in one hand and two sparkling black mugs emblazoned with his logo dangling from the fingers of the other.

"Twenty minutes, boss." She set the mugs and carafe down and handed him the file. "How you holding up?"

Hell, his pants threatened to split from the erection he now sported thanks to his meandering mind.

"Fine," he growled, grabbing the file and pulling it forward. "Let me know when they get here."

"'Kay," she replied.

Coop opened the folder and glanced over the proposal, though he knew every word by heart. He ought to—he'd written and re-read the damn thing at least sixty times.

Ginger cleared her throat and Coop dragged his gaze from the paper to his bleached-blond secretary. She twisted her fingers in front of her and was swaying back and forth like she'd had a shot of bourbon. Panic assailed him. She wasn't going to quit, was she? He'd never find anything in her mess of a filing system.

He half-rose. "What?"

She blew out a sharp breath. "I need the

evening off," she blurted out.

Coop grunted and fell back into his chair. "Ginger, we've been over this. I need you with me at the opera. The Gleasons—" He did not want to be mostly alone with Monica Gleason and her wandering fingers. Tactfully evading her advances was becoming harder and harder.

"I know and I'm so sorry." She leaned forward, planting her palms down on his desk, giving him the pleading puppy dog look. "But Rich asked me to stay the weekend with him at his parent's house."

"Go tomorrow. I need you tonight. Ginger, you know how important this is to the business."

She glared at him. "And you know how important Rich is to me. He wants me to meet his folks. This is *it*. I just know he's going to ask me to marry him."

Coop's panic rose again and he shoved it away. "Saturdays are the best days to meet potential in-laws."

"Coop, I'm going. Period."

"Damn it, Ginger."

"Damn it, Coop."

They glared at each other long and hard, until she finally sighed, seating herself on the edge of his desk. "I know how much this meeting means to you, boss, but take it from me, having your secretary at the opera is not going to clinch the deal."

"Quite right, my dear," an amused feminine voice drawled from the doorway.

Ginger squeaked and jumped up. Coop rose

and rounded the mahogany desk, a cautious smile on his face, hand extended to greet Troy and Monica Gleason. The future of his company. He'd spent many hours on the phone and at various events courting Troy Gleason, trying to get him to sign the deal, but the man was proving cautious. Coop needed him, needed the prestige that would elevate his company by having him as a client.

"Sorry there was no one to greet you out front." He gave Ginger a censorious glare.

She rolled her eyes and stalked from the office.

Monica waved away his words, ignored his outstretched hand and tilted her face for a kiss. His gut tightened and he looked quickly at Troy who just beamed. Coop brushed the older woman's pancaked face with a quick peck and drew hastily back, turning to her husband.

"Troy, good to see you. How are you?"

Troy Gleason was as heavyset and squat as a beer keg, but possessed one of the finest minds in business. Coop felt fortunate the man even deigned to consider working with him, much less the limited partnership he'd proposed. Taking Gleason's many interests and bringing them under one unified umbrella was a challenge, but Coop knew he was the man to do it. And once he did, his reputation, and his future, would be set.

"Fair to middlin'. Could complain, but I won't." Troy lumbered to one of the wide leather chairs in front of Coop's desk and settled his weight into it. Coop escorted Monica to the other one, waiting until she perched on the edge before rounding the desk and sitting himself.

"Monica was just telling me how much she was looking forward to tonight," Troy said, one brow raised. "You're not canceling on us just because you don't have a date, are you?"

Coop shuddered away at the very idea of dating Ginger. Jeez, she was like his little sister. "No sir, of course not."

"Excellent," Monica intoned in her smooth, modulated voice. "A threesome is so much more intimate, don't you agree?"

Coop's gaze briefly touched on Troy, checking to see if he'd caught the double entendre. From the smile on his face, he hadn't. Coop then assessed the inviting smile on Monica's perfectly shaded lips, paired it with the wealth of meaning she injected into the word *intimate* and got a nasty conclusion that beat against the back of his neck. Crap.

"Ginger isn't my girlfriend, she was just filling in as a favor."

Monica's eyes narrowed and Coop eased his chair back slightly. "Oh? I didn't know you were seeing anyone."

Troy chuckled and patted her hand. "Course you didn't, love, we're keeping him much too busy. And speaking of business, let's see your final proposal."

Coop wondered if the older man was totally blind and deaf, but decided not to mention his wife's pointed references. He slid the folder across the table.

"All of the financials are there, as well as the

projections and estimates for the next five years, which, as we agreed last week, would be the duration of our association."

"Provided all goes as planned," Troy said smoothly, settling a pair of silver-rimmed glasses on his face, leaning back and studying the paper intently.

Monica tapped her well-manicured nails against the shiny surface of his desk. "She's unable to join us tonight, then?"

Coop frowned. "Who?"

Her eyes narrowed slightly then a sly smile tipped up one corner of her mouth and her nostrils flared. She nodded as though they shared a special secret. "Your girlfriend, of course. What's her name?"

"Uh, her name?"

She licked her lips. "Yes."

Coop scrambled for a name, any name that sounded halfway feminine, but found himself coming up completely blank.

"Don't bother the man, Monica. We're here to work a deal, not his personal life." Troy tossed the file back to the desk. A frown creased his brow as he folded his glasses and stuffed them into his jacket pocket. "This all looks fine, but I'd like to get my attorney to read over the contract before I sign. He was supposed to join us today, but had a last-minute call to attend to."

Coop cursed silently, all the while maintaining a death grip on his smile. "Of course." But he really wanted to shout *sign the damn papers!* The sooner he could rid himself of Monica Gleason and her not-so-subtle innuendos, the better. He might have an eye for women, but God knew he'd never do a married woman. Strictly beyond his code of honor. He didn't know what he'd do if she actually made a move on him.

He didn't want to find out.

The Gleasons rose. Troy shook his hand firmly. Monica looked as though she wanted another kiss, but settled for a wink. "We'll pick you up at 6:30, Cooper."

"I'd still prefer to take my own car ."

"Nonsense," she spoke over him. "It will be much more convenient for us."

He nodded with reluctance. "All right. 6:30."

She waggled her fingers at him, latched onto Troy's arm and ushered him out of the office.

Coop remained standing, hands clenched into tight fists and shoved deep into his pants pocket. He heard Ginger wish them a good day and the click of the office door as she closed it behind them. Seconds later she appeared in his doorway.

A mischievous grin slanted across her mouth. "So? Did they sign?"

He snorted. "Like you don't know. You were hovering outside the door the entire time."

She laughed. "Yep." Ginger looked over her shoulder. "She sure has got some brass balls, doesn't she?"

Coop didn't need to ask. She might be young, but his secretary was wiser in the ways of the world than almost anyone he knew. Including himself. Sometimes she astounded him.

"Whatcha gonna do about tonight?"

Coop raked a hand through his hair then loosened the chokehold of his tie. "Hell, I don't know."

"Coop, if you really want me to go, I will."

"Nah, go to Rich's and meet his parents. I'll survive."

She giggled. "Cool. Okay, I'm outta here. It's almost three and I've still got to shop for some ultra-sexy lingerie."

Coop shook his head, hands held high. "Don't tell me, I don't want to know. Just go."

"Okay, boss. Night!" She whirled and in mere seconds he again heard the whoosh of the door opening over the carpet, then the click-clack of her heels in the tiled hallway as she left.

He sank into his chair, spun around to stare broodingly at the city skyline. He would survive.

He hoped.

He was never going to make it to intermission. If the awful, ear-splitting vocals didn't kill him, the hard seat beneath the overstuffed chair cushion would. Monica wouldn't have to do another thing. Coop shifted in his seat again, covertly looked at his watch and bit back a curse. Only five minutes later than the last time he checked. How the hell long did this crap go on, anyway?

It was an interminable twenty-two minutes

later that the chick in some flowing, golden gown flung her arms wide and screeched her last note. The curtain fell to thunderous applause.

As the house lights came up, Troy patted Monica's hand and rose. "Must run to the men's room, my dear. Believe I'll stop by the bar as well. May I bring you something back?"

She nodded. "White wine would be lovely."

"Malone, how about you?"

"Nothing, thanks," Coop said quickly, knowing one drink would probably make his already pounding head explode.

Troy left the box, closing the door behind him, shutting out the noise of people jamming the hallway during the intermission.

A hand trailed along his arm and he jumped, head whipping around. Monica had moved closer. Maybe he ought to change his mind about that drink. He eased back, but she followed.

"Too bad intermission only lasts fifteen minutes, Cooper." She chuckled throatily, her mouth coming dangerously close to his ear. He didn't need an interpreter to read her body language. Lately she'd become as subtle as a used car salesman. But he wasn't buying.

Monica wasn't a bad-looking woman. Her dark auburn hair suited her creamy complexion and he'd never seen her less than perfectly done up. Tall and athletic, she kept herself in very good shape. *With the help of a talented plastic surgeon.* A nip here, a tuck there and the boob job of a porn star. Coop much preferred supple, soft, real skin. Like his T-shirt wearing blond from Joe's. Gut instinct told him her tits were 100-percent God-given.

"Monica," he began gently, covering her hand with his, easing it off his arm. "This isn't right. Troy—"

"Oh, I know, lover." She winked and licked her lips. "Neither the right time nor place. We'll just have to make some plans. I know this wonderful, secluded bed and breakfast just outside of town."

Coop clenched his teeth briefly. If he came right out and told her he wasn't interested before he got Troy to sign those papers, would she demand her husband find another company to work with? He couldn't afford that. Sweat formed at the small of his back, making his linen shirt adhere to his skin. He'd sunk a ton of money into this venture. It couldn't fall through now.

But he wouldn't go to bed with her either. No way in hell would he sell his integrity to satisfy this horny she-devil.

He gave her a non-committal smile as he stood. "You know, I'd better find the men's room myself. I'd hate to miss any of the second act."

Monica's eyes flashed briefly before her gaze fell to the front of his crotch. "Need any help?"

"No," he said quickly. "I can handle it, thanks."

He turned and bolted from the room, heading upstream in the sea of returning patrons.

Finding the bank of elevators, he waited

while everyone else emerged before entering and randomly stabbing a button.

Monica's come-ons were getting worse. Bolder and more aggressive.

He had to get Troy to sign those papers. Once that was done, there would be nothing she could do if he told her to get lost. Politely, of course. He grinned as the sleek, chrome doors parted.

Stepping out, he realized he'd gone down too far. The walls were covered in flat gray paint and fluorescents flickered from the ceiling. Nothing like the plush burgundy carpeting and art deco light fixtures on the floors above.

Turning, he jabbed at the call button, shoved his hands in his pockets and jingled the change there while he waited. Coop looked at the display above the doors, sighing when he realized the elevator was still on the fourth floor.

A burst of laughter echoed down the hallway and he looked over his shoulder. A short man wearing a scowl and chomping on an unlit cigar pushed a door closed and ambled away from him, turning right into another door.

Coop checked the elevator again, finding it still stuck above. He wondered what was in the room the man had come out of. Curiosity, not to mention the delaying tactic, had him turning on his heel and making the short distance to a set of green double doors. *Employees Only* was emblazoned on them, but he figured a quick look wouldn't hurt.

Despite his distaste for tonight's performance

he'd always had a fondness for the stage, stemming from his many years in college drama. Though he was officially a techno geek, helping to run the lights and soundboards, he'd used his knack for organization and business savvy to help mold the department into a successful venture. Even then, he'd known he would make his mark in business. Acting was fun, business fueled him.

He checked his watch, realizing intermission wouldn't last much longer. Just one quick glimpse to see if it was still the way he remembered. Cracking open the door, he poked his head in.

People were everywhere, most of them in costume. Some stood in groups clutching cans and eating candy bars while others sprawled on the many couches and stuffed chairs littering the room. The smell of greasepaint, hairspray and stale coffee permeated the room. Except for the coffee, nothing changed. It was though he'd been transported back to college and opening night. He grinned, stepping into the room.

A melodious tone rang through the room and they sprang to life as though jolted with electricity, streaming out through a black door on the far side of the room. In less time than it took to blink, he stood virtually alone. The only other occupant was a petite woman with a mass of honey blond ringlets spilling down the back of the chair she occupied. For some reason those curls looked familiar, but he just couldn't place them. A deck of cards lay on the table beside her and she had her hand wrapped around a soda can.

"Excuse me," he said, stepping forward.

"Ack," the blond squeaked as she jumped up from the chair, whirling in one fluid motion. Coop couldn't decide if he was more impressed that she didn't spill any of her soda or by the voluptuousness of her breasts.

Her chest won, hands down.

"Sorry, I didn't mean to scare you," he said, moving closer.

Her mouth dropped open, then snapped shut audibly.

He squinted at her, walking to stand in front of her. "Don't I know you from somewhere?" Even as he said it, he realized she was his fetish from the coffee shop. Immediately his body threatened to respond. His gaze dropped briefly, skimming over the low-cut black shirt she wore tucked into equally black jeans.

"Uh…, uh…" A light rosiness colored her cheeks and her incredible silvery eyes were wide.

"You go to Cuppa Joe's, right? I've seen you there."

"You have?" Her voice emerged in a squeak and her eyes slammed shut then popped back open. "I mean, yes, I do. I've been a couple of times." She lifted the soda to her mouth and sipped.

"He's got great buns, doesn't he?"

She choked and coughed and Coop leapt forward, pulling the can from her hand and lightly rubbing and patting her on the back.

"Whoa, easy there."

The blond coughed a few more times, but her incredible gaze, though watery, firmly stuck to his. "I'm fine, thanks," she wheezed. "Um, swallowed wrong."

Coop nodded but found he couldn't pull his hand from the length of her back. Beneath the black T-shirt she wore, her skin was lean and enticing. His fingers stilled just below her shoulder blades, beneath the silken weight of her jasmine-scented hair.

Reaching out, he set the can on the table without letting go of her. He didn't want to let go and that shocked the hell out of him. Impulse was not high on his list of things to do, but something about her drew him in ways he couldn't explain. He felt odd, like he was trapped in a moment out of time where none of his usual rules applied.

"Why are you here?" she asked, one hand lifting, hovering above his chest.

Coop found himself wishing she would touch him. He pulled her closer, exhaling sharply when her breasts brushed against him.

"I'm not sure."

She licked her lips, her eyes dropping to his mouth.

Coop groaned. "I think I'm going to kiss you."

"God, I hope so," she said breathily, rising up on tiptoe, hands curving over his shoulders.

"You do?" he asked.

"Oh, yes, please."

Not one to argue, he covered her lips with his, taking her gasp in his mouth. She tasted like heaven and sin, catching him totally off-guard. Unable to resist, he deepened the kiss, sweeping his hands down the curve of her small waist and clutching at her hips. Soft lips, sweet tongue, delectable taste.

"Mmm." Her hands wrapped around his back and she responded wholeheartedly.

Coop lost himself in her lush mouth, savoring every new facet of this stranger. He had to keep kissing her. She was like a drug, screaming through his blood, instantly addictive.

"Am I interrupting something?" Monica's acid-laced voice echoed from the doorway.

The small woman in his arms froze then jerked away, silver-blue eyes wide and dazed. She tipped to the left, studied Monica for a moment then looked at him again.

He mouthed the word *help*, praying she'd go along with him, knowing no sane woman would.

"We have company."

Coop inhaled sharply as her husky, throaty voice rasped along his body with instant, if embarrassing, results. He glanced down, relieved his erection wasn't as apparent in his suit pants as it felt against his boxer briefs.

His gaze met hers again and she winked. She would go along with him. Relieved, he slowly turned around.

Monica stood near the door, icy fury on her face, fingernails tapping the wood paneling. "Monica," he said in his best surprised voice. "Is intermission over already?"

Monica's sharp green gaze shifted between him and the blond. She let the door close and stalked forward.

"Just about. You were gone so long, I became worried about you. Having once served on the advisory board, I'm familiar with the building, so I decided to look for you."

Monica was no longer looking at him, she was sizing up the small woman he'd just kissed. Coop looked at her as well, wincing a bit at the sight of her swollen, moist red lips. He'd not meant to be so rough.

"Aren't you going to introduce us?" Monica asked.

Oh, hell. He didn't know her name. "Uh, sure. Monica Gleason, this is –"

"Taryn Kirkpatrick." Taryn held out her hand, but Monica stared at it as though it was a dead snake.

"Charmed. Cooper," she turned to him, dismissing Taryn. "We must return to our seats."

The callous way she cut Taryn and the intimate emphasis she put on *our* grated on his nerves. He'd had just about all he could take from her.

"Has your husband found his way back?"

Monica's deeply rouged mouth twisted briefly before all expression fell from her face. "I imagine he has. Will your friend be joining us?"

"Nope," Taryn said cheerfully, wrapping a hand around his arm and brushing her magnificent breast against him. "Theatre people aren't supposed to go upstairs during a production."

A nasty, demeaning smile formed on Monica's lips. "I see. You're with the theatre. Not an actress, I presume?"

"Nope, I'm a costumer."

"How lovely. Cooper, we really must be going now, if we're to make it before the curtain rises."

"Why don't you go ahead and I'll catch up?"

"Oh, but you may not now the way back without me." She trilled piercingly, waving a hand with helpless innuendo. "Surely, Miss Kirkpatrick should return to work anyway."

"I should, Coop."

He jerked at her use of his name. Everyone who knew him called him that, except the Gleasons.

The low tone sounded in the room again and Taryn jumped. "Damn, I'm going to be late. And so will you, go on." She reached up on tiptoe and brushed a kiss to his cheek. "You'll come back down after the performance, won't you?"

Hell, yeah, he would. "Of course."

"But our car, Cooper. It doesn't do to have one's driver sitting around all night waiting. The poor man has a life of his own, you know."

The chastisement grated and he forced a civil smile. "Taryn can take me home."

"Absolutely," she breathed.

His pants twitched again. This was getting out of hand.

Monica's eyes iced over even more. Abruptly

she looked at Taryn. "Miss Kirkpatrick, we're having a small get-together at our country house this weekend. We were going to invite Cooper to join us. I would suggest you come as well, but I imagine you'll be working?"

Coop tensed, immediately alert. What the hell was she playing at?

Taryn hesitated and he didn't blame her. Kissed by a complete stranger, practically forced into taking him home and now an invitation to a party with a bunch of pretentious snobs she'd never met? She would be crazy to accept.

"Well," she cleared her throat, but he saw the gleam in her eye. "This happens to be my weekend off." She moved against him again.

Realizing Taryn knew how to play the game just as well as Monica, he relaxed slightly.

"I hate to be indelicate, but will we be sharing a room?"

Taryn's soft, provocatively-voiced words snapped any thoughts of relaxing out his head, causing certain parts of him to harden again.

Monica stared at them both, mouth slightly open. Finally, she nodded. "If that is what you want."

Taryn grinned, squeezing his arm. "Oh yeah, I definitely want."

Chapter Two

Cooper Malone. Her dream lover finally had a name. And he was one hell of a kisser. Taryn grinned widely, as she'd been doing off and on since the beginning of the second act, and it wasn't because of the show. Clutching a diaphanous gown to her chest, she closed her eyes and relived that delicious, incredible kiss again.

"Daydream on your own time!"

The harsh, strident voice of the lead soprano snapped Taryn away from the still-tingling memory of Coop's mouth on hers. She frowned at the brunette towering over her.

"Come on, you little twit, I need that gown. Quickly, quickly."

"Uh-oh," muttered one of the seamstresses around a mouthful of pins.

Though used to the high-maintenance and arrogant woman, Taryn's eyes narrowed. "Excuse me? A twit?" She slid the silky material through her fingers. One small cut was all it would take. "You want to go out there naked?"

"You want to keep your job?" the singer snarled, snatching at the costume.

"Knock it off, Taryn," Art Lasko, the stage manager, said with a growl.

Under the backstage lights, his bald head gleamed brightly. A half-smoked, mostly chewed stub of a cigar hung out of his mouth. "Trinee, go get dressed." He glared around the room. "Get back to work, people. Thirty more minutes and we're done. Thank God."

The cigar rolled from one corner of Art's mouth to the other while he favored her with an irritated scowl. "Two more weeks of performances and we get rid of her, Taryn. Can you behave that long?"

Taryn grinned. "Yeah, as long as she doesn't call me a twit again."

Art shook his head as he walked away.

The remainder of the show alternated between speeding by and crawling like a slug on fly paper. She tried to concentrate on the beauty of the music, the enraptured faces of the audience members and the glittering brilliance of the stage and costumes, but Coop always managed to get in the way.

She wasn't complaining.

The end finally arrived, the audience brought to its feet by Trinee's incredible vocals. The woman might be a first-rate bitch, but at least she had the talent to back it up.

Afterward, the usual mad, backstage scramble ensured. Costumes and props flew as the actors disrobed and dissected their performances.

Taryn kept an eye on the door to the green room as she gathered up the discarded clothing. Would he show?

And just who was that Monica woman anyway?

Art stomped into the room, gave his usual terse congratulations then a biting critique of things that needed improvement before dismissing them all for the night.

Anticipation had her nearly shaking in her velvet lace-up boots. She checked her watch. How long would it take the audience to clear out and Coop to make his way back down here?

Would he kiss her again? Maybe she ought to kiss him. And definitely cop a feel. She'd ogled his buns so long, she just had to know if they were as firm as they looked.

"Taryn, wanna grab a bite to eat?" a young man called out. "Bunch of us are heading over to Rosie's place for a late supper."

"No thanks, guys, I've got other plans tonight."

"Okay, next time. See ya."

As they left, the door behind her creaked open and she was filled by the giddiness of erotic anticipation. Oh yeah, she definitely wanted.

"Taryn?"

Cooper had come.

She chased the elation from her face. Turning to face him, she raked his tall form with a look she wished included x-ray vision. No, on second thought, she wanted to peel that black Italian silk suit from his broad shoulders herself. Wanted to unbutton each of the small closures lining his soft, white linen shirt and part it, so she could view his muscular chest.

Her gaze dropped lower and she licked her lips. One button, one zipper and —

"Taryn?"

Hearing the smile in his voice, she lifted her eyes, meeting his green-as-summer-grass stare head-on, barely suppressing a sigh of contentment. She could stare at him all day and find something new and fascinating, not to mention incredibly sexy and appealing, with every minute that passed.

"Hi." She waved one hand, engrossed by the deep dimples creasing his cheeks and bracketing his gorgeous, talented mouth.

"Hi."

Shaking herself from her stupor, Taryn tried to rein in her imagination, but it was hard. For too many hot nights she'd fantasized making love with this man and now, here he was in the flesh. And oh, what flesh it was.

Walking toward him, she smiled and held out her hand. "Guess we should formally introduce ourselves. I'm Taryn Kirkpatrick."

He chuckled, a rich, resonant sound that did funny things to her breathing. "Cooper Malone, nice to meet you. Thanks for saving me earlier."

Taryn raised a brow. "Well, lucky for you I'd not met my quota of kisses from handsome princes yet."

"And have you now?" His huskily-voiced question, paired with the leisurely but intent perusal he gave her body, sent more tingles zinging through her.

"Lord, I hope not." The words slipped out before she could stop them and for a brief second, Taryn was mortified. Despite their shared kiss and her imaginary romps with him, he was still a stranger. He didn't know her propensity for outrageousness.

Coop moved toward her, bringing with him the scent of expensive cologne. He smelled like one of those fold-back flaps in the fashion magazines. Normally they annoyed the hell out of her, but on him, it seemed absolutely perfect. One-hundred percent masculine and enticingly erotic.

Oh, boy.

Reaching up, he twined a curl of her hair around his finger, a wicked, inviting smile on his lips. "I hope not, either."

Taryn's usual wit deserted her, stolen by the hypnotic beauty of his eyes. Up close she saw the gorgeous green was flecked by bits of gold and framed by long, dark lashes.

She'd kill for lashes like that.

"Who," her voice cracked and she tried again. "Who was that woman and what did I save you from, anyway? She wasn't half-bad looking." Not half-good either, and much too old for him, despite the obvious visits to a plastic surgeon.

Coop's expression changed from flirtatious to guarded in a nanosecond. He moved a step away. "She's a corporate wife. I need her husband to sign on the dotted line and until I do,

I'm trying to avoid her advances."

Taryn narrowed her gaze. "And after he signs? Sounds like you plan on taking her up on her offer."

He reared back, shock on his face. "Hell, no! She's married, not to mention totally not my type."

She'd heard that one before. Been through the 'we're meant to be together' stage and wrung out by the 'I've outgrown your type' stage with her ex-husband.

Nibbling her bottom lip, Taryn debated her choices. She should give Coop the benefit of the doubt, right? After all, he was one magnificent hunk of man and if his real life bed skills were anything like her dreams, one night would be worth lowering her guard. Wouldn't it?

Her inner diva chastised her for the hesitancy. Men like Coop – sexy and fun instead of stodgy and predictable – mirrored her own, hard-won sense of self. A light romp without any complication was just what she was looking for.

Studying his face, she searched the tanned planes for sincerity, surprised to find it in the depths of his eyes and the wrinkle of his brow.

"Okay, sorry." She held up her hands. "I get a lot of exercise jumping to conclusions."

It was his turn to shrug. "Hey, you don't know me. Anything's possible."

The conversation faded into an awkward silence and Taryn mentally kicked herself for taking the flirtation from surface to entangled. *Damn, when will I learn?*

"So, you still want that ride home?"

His eyes met hers and he remained silent so long, she crossed her arms over her chest, an old habit she thought she'd long since outgrown. *Guess not.* "Well?"

"If you're still willing, I'd love one."

Coop's hand returned to her hair, sifting it through his fingers, sending waves of pleasure coursing through her entire scalp. She nearly purred aloud.

"Mmm," slipped from her. She watched him through half-open eyes, hoping he would kiss her again.

His lips parted and he focused on her mouth. "I have a problem, though." His voice was rough, intent.

"Yeah? What's that?" she asked breathlessly.

His fingers slid down her neck, palm flattening against the hollow of her collarbone. Her breasts responded to the proximity of his hand, swelling and throbbing with anticipation.

"I can only pay in kisses."

Taryn's breath hitched and her pelvic muscles contracted at the heated promise of his words. "I'm sure we can work out a deal."

His clasp tightened before he pulled away. "Good," he said huskily. "How about that ride?"

She knew what kind of ride she wanted from him. With a wicked smile, she nodded. "Okay, I'm out back. Hang on a sec."

Taryn locked all the doors in the green room except the one leading to the parking lot then turned off the lights. From the glow of the exit sign, she made out his tall form near the table and reached out, taking his hand in hers.

He had great hands. Strong, masculine, talented. She couldn't wait to see what they could do to her body.

Coop let her lead him through the room, enjoying her softness beneath his fingers. For a woman who worked with her hands, her skin was temptingly smooth. She nudged the door open with her hip and he stepped out into the still-sweltering Texas night. Almost midnight and he'd bet the thermometer hovered at ninety.

It was nothing compared to the fire his hormones had raging in him. What he was doing was absolutely crazy. Totally out of character for him and probably certifiable. She was a stranger. Granted, a beautiful stranger and one who frequented the same coffee shop he did, but that didn't mean she was safe.

If he had any sense, he'd run like hell. But, to his shock, one taste of her hadn't been enough. He needed, craved more. Through the remainder of the opera he'd envisioned her in a variety of positions, all of them naked. And in his bed. Except the one where she'd been bent over the arm of his leather couch.

"Here I am."

With difficulty he shook himself out of his sensual imaginings and stared first at the red and black Harley in front of him, then the helmet she held out.

"You ride a motorcycle?"

Her grin flashed saucily under the hazy orange parking lot lights. "Yep. It's a '93 Heritage Softail."

She leaned close and he bent his head, immediately surrounded by her scent of spicy musk mingled with greasepaint.

"One of these days, I'll tell you why I ride my Harley." With a wink and sultry laugh, she turned back to the bike, unlocking one of the saddlebags and pulling out a set of chaps. "Sorry I don't have a pair for you to wear. I didn't know I'd need extra protection tonight." Another wink, another low, libido-raising chuckle.

Coop couldn't have responded if he'd had a brain to do it with. She'd taken his breath and his voice by strapping the black, leather chaps around her curvaceous hips. The material framed her pert, nicely rounded bottom, making his hands itch to cup it.

Leather. He altered his earlier fantasy, now visualizing Taryn bent over his couch, wearing only those black leather chaps.

Oh, God.

With a silent groan, he moved the helmet to his crotch. How the hell was he going to ride that bike without poking her in the back with his now raging hard-on?

From her back pocket she took out a pack of gum. She popped one of the cinnamon flavored sticks in her mouth and offered him a piece, but he declined. He was hot enough right now.

After pulling on a black jacket, leather of course, Taryn hopped on the bike and patted the seat behind her. "Mount up, cowboy."

Not the best words to use right now. He'd like to mount something and it sure as hell wasn't a damn motorcycle. Gritting his teeth, Coop settled the helmet on his head and slung his leg over the bike. A small, plastic wrapped wire hung over the side of his helmet and he wondered what it was.

"Where we going?"

He gave her directions to his house and she turned to grin at him.

"Really? That's close to me." That alluring laugh again. "Duh, so is Joe's."

So, she did recognize him from Joe's. He shouldn't have been surprised, but he was. Why in the world would a good-looking, wild woman like her notice a straight-laced guy like him?

Taryn straddled the Harley, both boot-clad feet on the ground and twisted her hair into some kind of fuzzy knot then put on her own helmet.

"Better hold on, Coop."

Her melodious voice sounded in his ear and he realized the wire was actually a microphone. Hold on? He stared at her back, gaze drifting down to her butt. Nice.

"To what?" he asked.

"To me. Put your arms around my waist."

The engine started with a loud rumble and he complied, his hold light. He didn't want to hurt her.

"Harder, Coop."

"Ah, damn," he groaned at her choice of words, but tightened his grasp. The bike roared forward, streaking from the parking lot and onto the quiet downtown street in half a second.

Coop felt like he left his stomach back at the

opera.

"You okay?"

"Great," he muttered, closing his eyes to shut out the light posts whizzing by. He'd never been on a motorcycle and now he knew why. Apparently he had motion sickness.

Thankfully the ride eased out about the time they hit the freeway, though going up the entrance ramp had him queasy as hell. Once on smoother ground, his stomach settled down and he was able to open his eyes.

Not a good idea, so he stared at the back of her helmet, noticing for the first time the voluptuous silver devil etched into the black plastic. Slung back in a seductive pose, she winked naughtily at him, raising all kinds of thoughts.

Taryn was sexy as hell, a great kisser, a good sport and a biker babe. Totally out of his realm of experience. Remembering Monica's weekend invitation, he wondered how Taryn would fit in, knowing she couldn't possibly. What would a woman like her say to the high-brows that ran in Monica's circle?

"You always this quiet?"

"Yeah, pretty much," he said.

Her sigh drifted through his helmet. "The strong, silent type, huh? I like that."

Coop stroked her leather jacket, inching upward. Her breasts were so close. One good jar from the road and he'd easily brush against them. "What else do you like?"

"Hang on, I'm gonna lean left a little. You stay straight."

"Huh?"

The bike slowed and he looked up, relieved to find them nearing Joe's. He wondered if he'd suffered permanent damage from the engine's vibrations running up his spine.

"We need to turn, so I lean left a bit, you stay still."

The bike took the corner flawlessly, without so much as a bump or skid. He had to admit Taryn handled the motorcycle with confidence and ease. He wondered how long she'd been riding.

They passed the coffee shop. "Okay, you'll need to direct me from here," she said.

"Left at the light, second right, third house on the left. You can park in the driveway."

"Got it."

In under two minutes she pulled up in front of his house, killed the engine and took off her helmet. Coop didn't immediately let go of her waist, enjoying the feel of her moving underneath the leather.

A guy could develop a fetish this way.

When she turned to him, he reluctantly let go and lifted his helmet off.

Unzipping her jacket, she regarded him steadily, a small smile on her lips. "You might want to be careful getting off."

Coop raised a brow before raking her with a long, meaningful glance. "Yeah? Why's that?"

She chuckled and held her hand out. "Down, boy. First, hot pipes, they burn like a Son-of-a-bitch." She grinned. "And it's kinda like sea legs. If you're not used to riding, you might have some difficulty finding your balance."

Great, just what he needed. Fall on his face like an idiot while this sprite of a woman handled the heavy bike like it was a ten-speed.

Coop gritted his teeth and swung his leg over the black seat. With false confidence he settled his feet on the pavement and stood. His knees threatened to buckle and his thighs shook, but he stayed upright.

He grinned at her. "See, I'm fine."

Taryn shook her head, curls bouncing and swaying around her heart-shaped face. Sliding off the bike, she stood in front of him. "I agree, but can you walk?"

Lord, he hoped so, but he wasn't ready to try. And he wasn't quite ready for her to climb on her Harley and roar off into the night either. He grimaced, hoping the neighbors didn't get onto him about the noise.

Coop folded his arms over his chest, surreptitiously leaning against the seat for support. "You never told me what else you like, Taryn."

She didn't say anything for a long moment, just stared at him, pulling her silver gum wrapper from her pocket, lifting it to her mouth. He caught a glimpse of her tongue as it slid out, depositing the cinnamon gum then swiping across her lips. He swallowed hard.

Who knew gum could be so erotic?

The wrapper disappeared into her pocket and she mimicked his stance. "What do you like?"

He grinned. "I asked you first."

"Yep, you sure did. Think you can walk

now?"

With a laugh, he moved forward, sliding his arms around her waist. "Yeah."

Taryn braced her palms against his chest, looking up at him with her piercing silver-blue eyes. "I can see that."

"So, you ready for me to pay up?"

She licked her lips, her gaze falling to his mouth. The blatant act jolted through him, ending with a sizzle at his crotch.

"Maybe."

Lowering his head, Coop nuzzled the soft curls at her temple. She was driving him crazy, making him irrational. He never did this kind of crazy thing. He sure as hell had never propositioned a perfect stranger before. It both excited and annoyed him, but he was helpless to stop it. "How much do I owe you? Wait." He stilled her words with a finger, caressing the soft moistness of her lower lip. "Why don't we take this negotiation inside?"

Her eyes widened and she jerked in his arms. "We need to talk about this party, Coop."

"I like the way your mouth purses when you say my name. Perfectly round and very inviting."

She smacked his shoulder lightly. "Stop that. I'm serious. We need to talk about it. I have some idea of what to expect, but I'd like confirmation."

"Can I pay for my ride first?"

The deep breath she took forced her full breasts against his chest. Reflexively he pulled her a fraction closer. Oh yeah, 100-percent real and all woman. What would she feel like in his hands? Silky, smooth, heavy and luscious. Like a ripe melon. He sucked in a breath, reining himself in as much as he could. It wasn't easy. "Taryn?" he managed.

"Okay," she said. "One kiss."

"Just one? How about five?" he countered.

"Five's a bit steep." She grinned. "Not to mention a possible fire hazard. Two."

Coop chuckled. "Two is cheap and I'm fire-proof. Four."

"Hmm." She traced the pleated pattern of his shirt just above where her nipples rested against him. When she shrugged, his fingers spasmed around her waist, digging into the taut flesh. "I'm a risk-taker by nature, you know."

He held his breath. "And?"

Her hands inched up his shoulders, slipped under his jacket. "I'm willing to risk three."

"Hot damn."

As Coop lowered his head, she tightened her grip on him and leaned forward, her mouth coming up to meet his. He brushed her lips once, twice. Soft, heady kisses, meant to refresh his senses with her taste and shape.

Taryn was having none of it. Her hands tangled in the hair at the base of his neck, pulling him to her.

A groan escaped him and he forgot slow, aiming straight for deep and intense. She tasted spicy and racy, welcoming and heated. Her mouth opened under his and he swept inside, seeking out her tongue with his, demanding a response.

Taryn was uninhibited, wild, giving and just as demanding as he. Coop's world tipped and tumbled, the only stability this hot woman and her incredible, hot mouth.

Only when his lungs threatened to burst did he reluctantly pull away. They both gasped for breath.

In the glow of the bright August moonlight, Coop traced her swollen lips with his thumb, chagrined to see he was shaking. Taryn also trembled in his arms like a leaf in a thunderstorm. She managed a smile.

"That's one."

Chapter Three

Cooper Malone was one hell of a kisser and if she didn't watch out, Taryn knew she'd get burned. Again. But even the murmur of that warning wasn't strong enough to make her pull her mouth away from his talented lips.

One kiss had only whetted her appetite. This second one nearly seared her eyeballs in their sockets. She shivered in delicious anticipation of what a third would do.

"Maybe we should take this inside," Coop suggested again, his voice rough and husky, as though she'd taken his breath away.

Taryn liked that thought. Liked the idea that she had any kind of power over this strong, masculine hunk of man.

"Hmm," she pretended to ponder. "It's awfully late, Coop. I really should be getting home."

He growled and pulled her tighter against him. His hands spanned her waist, creeping underneath the leather jacket and smoothing the crushed velvet of her white tee.

"I still owe you two kisses."

"Yes, you do." She pulled away from him, rational thinking finally breaking through the sensual web he'd woven around her. "But we need to talk as well. And," she pressed her fingers to his protesting mouth. "I have a feeling we'd get no talking done if we went inside. Kissing, yes." She smiled wryly. "Talking no."

"Kissing is good." His wicked, come-hither grin made her heart thump quickly and her lower body tingle even more. "Kissing you is damn good."

Taryn chuckled. "Yeah, you're not so bad yourself. However," she pulled out of his grasp entirely, relieved and a bit disappointed when he let her go, "we need to set some ground rules, especially if I go to Monica's house party with you."

Coop's demeanor changed as quickly as the Texas weather. Raking a hand through his hair, he closed his eyes, jaw muscles bunching.

He looked like he was in great pain.

He sighed harshly. "I don't know about that, Taryn. I don't think it's such a great idea."

She lifted a brow. "Oh? Why not?"

His struggle to find the right words did not impress her, especially since she just *knew* what he was thinking. It couldn't be any different than anything her ex-husband had ever told her. She didn't fit in with those kinds of people. She was not refined enough. Not classy enough. *Too much Marilyn, not enough Jackie.*

Well, she didn't have to take any crap off her ex anymore and she sure as hell didn't have to take it from this kiss-stealing Neanderthal in a suit. Taryn clenched her fists.

"Look, bucko—"

"I don't want them to hurt you."

"Huh?" Realizing her mouth was hanging open, she snapped it shut. "What are you talking about?"

Coop shrugged, shoving his hands into his pockets and rocked back on his heels, clearly uncomfortable. "Those kinds of women, well, they can be... that is, they're sometimes —"

"Bitches?" she finished for him.

He nodded. "I just know they'd gang up on you. Try to make you feel unwanted. Hurt you."

Taryn bit her bottom lip, surprised he would be so aware of the guerilla maneuvering of society women. His concern was touching, if unnecessary. But he didn't know she was more than capable of taking care of herself with those female sharks. He didn't know her.

Time to change that, at least in the carnal way. Taking what she wanted had become a familiar mantra for her, be it shoes, purses or clothes. Why not men? Celibacy sucked anyway and she'd bet her Harley he would blow her mind in bed, among other things.

"I can take care of myself, Coop, but I think you'll have to find that out for yourself."

"I don't doubt it, but still..." He shrugged again.

"Look, let's talk about this later, okay? It's been a really long day for me and we've got three more performances to get through. I don't have to be at the opera until three on Monday.

Will you be free for lunch?"

Coop nodded. "Sure, I'd love to have lunch with you. I should be caught up. I'm working in the office tomorrow."

"In on a Saturday?" Damn, a familiar sign…her ex had been a workaholic.

"Yeah, need to catch up. The Gleasons are important clients, but I've got others and need to look over some stuff while the phones aren't ringing off the wall. I hate working Saturdays though. I'd rather be doing anything else."

Taryn brightened with the news. "Where do you work?"

"My office is just off Airport Freeway."

Taryn took the business card he handed her, not even trying to make out the writing in the pale moonlight. "Okay, I'll pick you up at noon?"

"Uh," he turned to glance sourly at her bike. "You can come to my office, but how about I drive?"

She laughed. "Deal."

The clicking cicada serenade and chirping cricket chorus folded around them as they stared at each other. Taryn let her gaze fall to his lips, wanting desperately to have another taste, yet afraid to allow herself the pleasure.

One more kiss and what small shred of caution she still claimed would be tossed aside like last week's leftovers and she'd find herself in his bed. Not necessarily a bad thing, but she didn't want him to think her totally easy.

Her breath quickened. A faint flicker of a memory from one of her dreams darted in and out of her mind's eye. Clearly she saw him above her, sweat streaked jaw clenched in orgasm.

"Damn," she muttered, resolve wavering.

"What's the matter?"

"I gotta go." If she stayed… well he was just a little too tempting. Stomping past him, she straddled the bike and slapped her helmet on, jerking the chin strap harder than necessary. The leather bit into the soft flesh of her throat and she growled in disgust as she loosened the strap.

"Taryn?" He stood next to her, concern on his handsome face.

Quit with the nice guy thing. It would be so much easier to leave if he were an ass with an ego the size of King Kong. But so far he'd exhibited none of those traits.

"Night, Coop."

The bike started, growling its distinctive rumble into the night. She lifted her hand in farewell. He clasped her fingers, stopping her. Taryn looked up at him.

Before she could blink, his mouth found hers again, weakening her resolve. The powerful vibrations of the motorcycle between her legs only heightened the instant desire he sparked. She pressed her thighs around the curved black seat and let herself fall into him again.

Coop lifted his head, smiling devilishly. "That was good night. I still owe you two."

He stepped away and Taryn somehow managed to get the bike down the driveway and onto the street without tipping it. What was he doing to her? With a roar, she pealed off into the night.

She had to fortify her defenses.

Make a plan to take on Mr. Malone.

Find the perfect outfit for Monday.

Fifteen minutes to go. Coop bounced the eraser of his pencil up and down on his desk, watching the minute hand inch around the chrome clock on his wall.

Inch, nothing, more like centimeter. Millimeter.

"Whatcha doin', boss?" Ginger snapped her gum as she waltzed into his office.

"Reading." He looked down at the open file in front of him, not seeing a word of the proposal. All he saw was the way Taryn's skin had glittered underneath the moonlight. The way her breasts filled out her t-shirt so well it simply had to be illegal. The way her mouth tasted and melted under his.

"Great, so you'll give me my nine mil a year raise?"

"Yeah, whatever you need," he murmured, barely registering her words.

She sighed and plopped her butt down on his desk, nearly upending his coffee cup.

She waved her hand in front of his face. "Hellooooo, Coop. What's up with you?"

Snapping back from his sensual daydream he raised his gaze. Damn, she had that meddling, I'm-going-to-figure-it-out look. "It's called work, maybe you've heard of it?"

Her eyes narrowed and a quirky grin lifted her lips. He suppressed a groan.

"I smell a woman!"

"Who's watching the front office?"

"I can see from here. So, spill. Who is she? Where did you meet her?"

Gritting his teeth, Coop sought a way to get his nosy secretary out of his office and back to her desk. Nothing short of dynamite came to mind. And he wasn't even sure that would work.

"You don't know her."

Ginger pouted. "You've met a woman and you don't want to tell me about her? After all we've been through? I tell you everything about my boyfriends."

"I know," he said dryly. She missed the sarcasm altogether.

"C'mon, Coop, don't keep me in suspense."

He lifted his cup to his mouth, hiding his grin behind a sip of coffee. Driving her crazy would pass the time until Taryn arrived. He checked the clock again. Nine minutes, twenty seconds.

Ginger slipped from her perch, whirled and flattened her palms against his desk. "Don't make me fight dirty, Coop," she threatened softly. Her grin was pure hell-raiser.

He swallowed the dark brew and narrowed his eyes. He didn't like the sound of that. "What do you mean?"

She straightened, smoothing her hair and tugging the jacket of her bright orange suit down. She nodded. "I'll call your mother."

"Shit."

"Tsk, tsk, Mr. Malone, such language."

"Shut up, Ginger." He sighed, knowing he'd been beat. The last thing he needed was for his mom to hear about this. She'd have him married and naming a dozen grandkids inside a week. "Her name is Taryn and I met her at the opera."

Ginger's brows knitted even as she smiled smugly. "The opera? The same opera you attended with Grabby Gleason?"

"Uh-huh."

Ginger whistled. "And how did she take that?"

"Not well," said a husky, feminine voice from the doorway.

Coop shot to his feet, excitement pounding through him with the force of a roller coaster.

"Taryn, you're early."

"Want I should leave and come back?" Amusement rippled in her voice.

Hell, no. "Please, come in."

Coop watched as she sauntered into the room, moving with sinuous grace. Her blond hair curled around her face in leonine fashion and her silver-blue eyes seemed to stand out even more against the smoky dark eye shadow she wore. His gaze dropped to her mouth. He planned on kissing that coppery lipstick off the first chance he got. He felt in his back pocket for his handkerchief.

"Hi, I'm Ginger."

He studied Taryn while she talked with Ginger, not even caring that every word and every detail would soon land in his mother's ears. Today Taryn wore a white button-up shirt with a wide, stand-up collar, a low square neckline that perfectly showed off the shadow of her cleavage and long sleeves that flared at the wrist. Exquisitely feminine.

She'd tucked the shirt into a pair of black slacks and when she shifted, he saw what looked to be a leather band, bound by silver grommets running down each leg.

Black stiletto boots completed her outfit. While she looked beautiful and sexy, his gut clenched just thinking of taking her to Monica's and allowing those female sharks to get their teeth into her.

Much as he hated the idea, he had to find a way to get her to change her mind about going.

"Taryn, you ready?"

She nodded. "That would be great, Ginger. Here, give me a call whenever you'd like to go."

"You bet!"

Coop slid his arm around Taryn's waist and gently nudged her out the door. "Go where?" he murmured, breathing in her subtle, spicy perfume.

Taryn slanted him an amused glance. "Out. I told Ginger about this great little bar I know. Excellent house band, full buffet and a decent-sized dance floor."

He rubbed his thumb along her hip. "Sounds fun."

She laughed. "Somehow I don't quite see it as your kind of place."

Steering her toward the elevator, he pushed the down button then shoved his hands in his pockets, frowning. "Why not?"

Her brow wrinkled and her lips pursed slightly, nearly making him forget his question.

"It's pretty much a dive. You won't find any up-and-coming businessmen or professionals there. Just a bunch of artists and musicians. Bohemians, my mom calls us."

The elevator doors parted and they stepped in, making the swift ride to the parking garage in silence. He led her to his sparkling silver Lexus and opened the door, waiting until she'd slid onto the mahogany-colored leather seat.

Bohemian. The word kicked around in his gut like he'd eaten a dozen sour jawbreakers. Monica and her crowd would eat Taryn alive. "So, that's the kind of people you usually hang out with?"

"Mostly, yes. Where are we going?"

"A great little Italian place just up the street. Nice atmosphere and even better food."

"Sounds good."

Coop wanted to ask more about her friends, her lifestyle, her. The need to seek out and expose every delectable part of Taryn Kirkpatrick continued to beat at the back of his mind. "How long have you lived here?"

"All my life."

Her hand was still on his arm, rubbing slow, soft circles. It felt good. Natural.

"How long is that?" he asked, tossing her a grin.

Her gold-tipped nails bit gently into his forearm. "Don't you know it's not polite to ask a woman her age?"

"Sure do. So, how old are you?"

Taryn's laughter filled the car. She didn't hold back, didn't emit one of those silly giggles or fake, ladylike sounds that were supposed to be amusement. He liked the way it sounded.

"I'm twenty-eight, how old are you?"

"Thirty-three." He pulled into the parking lot and killed the engine. "Stay there, I'll get your door."

Surprised but pleased that she didn't argue, Coop escorted her up the flagstone walk and into the cool, vine covered foyer of the restaurant.

The hostess, dressed in the uniform black pants and white ruffled shirt, led them through a maze of mostly occupied tables. Once they were seated, she told them their waitress would be right with them.

Coop barely had time to pick up the menu when a similarly-clad young girl who looked like she should be in high school appeared to take their drink orders.

Taryn opted for a soda, he chose ice tea and recommended the shrimp scampi and pasta when she asked.

Her throaty chuckle brought his head up. "As long as I'm not the only one with shrimp and garlic breath."

Reaching over, he twined their fingers, rubbing her knuckles. "I happen to find garlic very sexy."

Shaking her head, she sipped at her drink. "So, you're not a vampire, but you are a hard one to peg, Cooper Malone."

He was surprised. Most women, hell most

people, immediately identified him as a stuffed shirt, a nose-to-the-grindstone, straight arrow kind of guy. In other words, boring. Never hard to peg.

It took time and energy to build a successful company from the ground up. Every resource, almost every spare moment he had, he'd devoted to Malone, Inc. Sure, he'd had a few dates, even sex now and again, but nothing serious. Nothing to take away from the business. Staring across the table into Taryn's beautiful face he realized how much he wanted that to change. How much he wanted her.

"Really?" He squeezed her fingers then leaned back. "Why's that?"

"Playing coy?" she teased.

He snorted. "Hardly. Are you sure you're out with the same guy I see in my mirror in the morning?"

Her pink tongue peeked out, swiping across her top lip in a slow, erotic arc. "I'd have to see him for myself to be sure."

Coop leaned forward. "That is easily arranged."

"Speaking of arrangements…"

"Yeah?" He moved out of the waitress' way as she set his shrimp in front of him.

"What's the dish with your client's party this weekend?" Taryn sniffed at her plate, smiling across the garlic-scented steam at him. "You think you'll be able to seal the deal?"

"I get the feeling this is more of a test for me than anything."

She scowled. "From Monica? Or Mr.

Gleason?"

"Maybe both," he paused, not wanting to just spill his suspicions about Mrs. Gleason's intentions. "Well, Monica is Monica and I think Troy wants to see if I can hold up under social pressure."

"Well, I'm happy to do anything I can to keep you out of her clutches, you poor innocent man."

He laughed, shaking his head. "I can hold my own, Taryn."

"I'm sure you can." Taryn popped a shrimp in her mouth, eyes widening at the succulent flavor. "Wow, this is really good."

"Did you doubt me?" he teased, his green eyes warm and friendly.

Shaking her head, Taryn continued to smile. "I don't even know you, how can I doubt you? Which brings us to this weekend."

He raised a hand. "Can we talk about that later? I'd rather talk about you."

She clutched her fork before forcing her fingers to relax. "I'm just your average girl."

Coop gave a sharp crack of laughter that had heads turning. "You, Miss Kirkpatrick, are anything but average."

His sincerity was obvious. Warmth flooded her, pooling in her stomach. "Thanks."

"How did you become a costumer?"

She relaxed slightly, enjoying the meal, the atmosphere, but most of all, Coop's company and the constant surge of desire she saw in his eyes. It had been so long since a man had looked at her with that kind of hunger. "More of my bohemian nature, I'm afraid. I went to college to study international business and marketing, made it through two years before I fell into this by accident. Met a guy at a party. He was in the theatre department and introduced me to the art and history of costuming. I signed up for one class and was hooked. Changed my major, stayed in school an extra year then landed a few jobs here and there before the opera hired me."

One of his dark brows quirked upward, giving him a roguish, enticing look. "That was a quick ten years."

Taryn bit into another shrimp, debating. She dabbed at her lips with her napkin, holding his steady gaze. "Well, I did do one other thing during that time."

"Spent some time in jail?" he teased.

"No." She scowled.

He held up his hands. "I'm playing, honest. So, tell me, what did you do?" He pushed his plate away, leaning his elbows on the table, spearing her with an intense emerald stare.

Suddenly she felt uncertain. That hadn't happened to her in at least two years. Her throat seemed parched, her lips dry. A long, cooling drink of her soda cured the feeling but did nothing for her uncharacteristic nervousness.

"Taryn? You okay?"

His deep voice carried across the table, easily heard over the clink of silverware and muted chatter of the other diners. With effort, she shook off the heckling ghosts of her past. "Yes, sorry. I zoned, I suppose." She traced the rim of her glass, forcing herself to look him in the face. "I got married."

Shock quickly followed by resignation washed over his face. His eyes narrowed and his brows furrowed darkly. "I see."

"No, you don't. I also got divorced."

The harshness melted in an instant. "I'd say I'm sorry, but I'd be lying."

The tightness that gripped her eased somewhat. "Thanks, I'm not sorry either." Taryn grinned before licking a droplet of garlic butter off her finger. Noticing the rapt way he watched, she couldn't resist a bit of teasing. Sucking until her cheeks began to hollow, she drew her finger out slowly, releasing it with a soft pop.

He groaned. "Do you know what you are doing to me, Taryn?"

"I hope like hell you're hard as all get out under those snazzy slacks of yours."

"And then some."

"Excellent." She chuckled, leaning back in her chair. "What about you? Ever take the plunge?"

"Nah, never any time. Since I finished college I've worked hard at building my business."

"And just what do you do?"

"I'm a troubleshooter in organizational management."

She blinked. "Which is what?"

"I consult with businesses, look at their structures and operating systems and show them how to streamline, organize and generally become more profitable. Most of the time without the need to lay anyone off."

"Wow, I'm impressed."

Coop shrugged. "Don't be. I sort of lucked into it. I worked for my uncle's hotel for a while. I'd see an area he could improve on and suggest it. Then another. Then another, well you get the picture."

"Yep. So, where do the Gleasons fit into all this?"

"A lot of my business is referral-based. The Gleasons own many different companies that do different things. They want to pull all the operating systems under one umbrella and they're looking to me to help them consolidate. I hope."

Taryn liked the spark in his eyes when he spoke about his business. He was passionate, there was no denying that. Hell, the way he kissed he couldn't be anything but passionate. However, he also belonged to a world she'd walked away from long ago. She toyed with the condensation dripping down her glass. "And the party this coming weekend? You said you think it's a test?"

Coop leaned forward, slipping his fingers through hers. "Yeah. I've heard the Gleasons are big on appearances and stuff. A bit too high-brow snobbery for my tastes, but this deal will absolutely seal my future."

She tensed. "Appearances? Like what? No shirt, no shoes, no contract?"

"Nah, more like can I mingle comfortably with their circle." He cleared his throat.

"Though, probably showing up in jeans and a leather jacket would not endear me to them."

Fire flared in her gut. "You're saying I should leave the Harley at home?"

His fingers tightened around hers and he looked away for a moment, before his green eyes bore into hers. "I'm saying that what they think and what is reality are two different things."

"Rich people are always like that, Coop. It's fed into them on their silver spoons." She narrowed her gaze. "Are you uninviting me? Worried that I might embarrass you?"

"No," he stated loudly. "I said it before Taryn, I'm worried about the damage they'll do to you. Having money doesn't always mean having manners."

Overlooking the relief his words stirred, she studied his clean, strong jaw and sensuous lips. A snippet of last night's dream flashed brilliantly through her mind and she sucked in a deep breath. She wanted to be spread out on his bed, clutching that talented mouth to her clit, crying out her orgasm. The opportunity to fulfill her fantasy and ease the perpetual ache she'd been fighting was too good to pass up. If it meant hobnobbing with a bunch of society witches, so be it. "Look Coop, I appreciate the sentiment, but I told you, I can take care of myself. I won't embarrass you and I won't make you lose this deal. But if I don't go, Monica is sure to try something. What happens if her husband finds her in your bed?"

"She won't be there, I guarantee it."

Taryn licked her lips and infused as much seductive pleading in her voice as possible. "Let me come, Coop."

Chapter Four

"Think of it as being fashionably late," Taryn murmured as Coop pulled his silver car up to the circular driveway of the Gleasons' house. This was a country house? She'd seen smaller apartment complexes.

"I hate being late, fashionably or otherwise," he said tightly.

The valet opened her door and she stepped out, catching Coop's eyes over the roof of the car. "Relax, okay? It's how the game is played."

He popped the trunk and stalked to the back. She could tell by his heavy footsteps he was not pleased. Joining him at the rear of the car, she reached for her two small suitcases.

"I'll get them. And it's not a game, okay? This is my life, my career, we're talking about here."

Stung, she fell back and turned to look at the house again. Huge and purposefully imposing, the white Colonial screamed wealth and prestige. A knot formed in her stomach that refused to budge. What the hell had she been thinking to come here? Her body was ruling her and it needed a serious refresher course in blatant idiocy.

His hand curved around her shoulder with a gentle touch. "I'm sorry, Taryn, I didn't mean to snap at you."

With a sigh, she turned and swallowed her pride for what she hoped would be the last time this weekend. "No, you were right, Coop. It's not a game. I made you a promise and I won't go back on it. Everything will be fine. I'll behave and the Gleasons will have absolutely nothing but wonderful things to say about you."

Worry lines etched grooves in his cheeks where his dimples usually flashed. Reaching up, she smoothed her fingertips over his skin then brushed a kiss against his mouth, savoring the freedom to do so. "Relax. Mingle. Take the time to make new contacts. We'll be fine."

His frown eased as he drew in a deep breath and a hint of spark returned to his green eyes. "Relax, huh? Somehow I don't think that'll be possible, I stay perpetually rigid around you."

She laughed and glanced down then back up with a quick wink. "Don't worry, we'll take care of that later, Coop. For now, let's go inside, find our room and get ready for the pre-dinner cocktail hour that's already in swing."

He raised a dark brow. "How do you know what's going on?"

Picking up her bags, she tipped her head toward the wide front doors. "Trust me."

He studied her intently before nodding. "I already am, Taryn."

His shoulders relaxed and the frown worrying his brow abated. The smile he gave her appeared genuine and less tense. Thank goodness. The stranger who'd swept her into a mind-numbing, spontaneous kiss didn't seem the kind to be repressed and rigid.

Well, not rigid in that way. Other ways were delectably encouraged.

She grinned back. "Come on, let's go check out the bed."

"Oh lord." He laughed and started forward. "Sounds good to me." And like that, they were good again.

They barely made it to the stairs when the door opened and two men dressed in black slacks, white shirts and tasteful dove-gray vests stepped out. "Mr. Malone, Miss Kirkpatrick. Your room is ready." They took the bags and turned. "This way, if you please."

Taryn swallowed against the sudden dryness of her throat, grateful when Coop pressed his warm hand to the small of her back and guided her forward. She sensed she would need his strength to keep her grounded the entire weekend. Could she do this again?

Yes, damn it. This is different. He's not William, these people are not in politics and I'm a totally new woman. The opinions of the narrow-minded meant nothing to her anymore and if they didn't like the way she looked or dressed, tough shit.

Taryn focused on Coop by her side and briefly glanced at the lush appointments of the entryway, the huge oil portraits lining the wide staircase they ascended. What she'd seen so far only emphasized the fact that these people had money and power. Two things she'd been divorced over.

The servants entered a door at the end of a long hallway and set their bags down near the bed. The younger man nodded and left while the elder stayed behind, opening the drapes and flipping on lights, explaining where everything was.

Taryn hoped Coop was paying attention because her entire being was focused on the sumptuous king-sized bed that occupied the far side of one wall. Dressed in royal blue and piled high with fat, satin-covered pillows, it was a feast for the eyes.

She licked her lips, knowing that later it would prove a different kind of feast—one of sensual exploration and pleasure. Fingers shaking with anticipation, she pushed her curls back behind her ear and smiled up at Coop. He winked back.

"The guests are downstairs in the yellow salon enjoying cocktails when you are ready." The man tipped his head and walked to the door.

"What's your name, please?"

He stopped, one hand on the door and gave her a quizzical look. "Brent, ma'am."

Taryn smiled. "Thank you for your help, Brent."

"Most welcome, ma'am," he replied cheerfully. Nodding again, he left them alone.

Coop moved to the bed, looking over his shoulder at her as he tested the firmness with a strong push. "Sturdy," he said with a grin. "I have a feeling that's a good thing."

Taryn laughed and he found himself enchanted all over again. Her silver-blue eyes gleamed with her humor and her luscious mouth beckoned him. "You think so, huh, Tiger?"

He crooked his finger at her. "Yep. Come here, Taryn."

Shaking her head, she smiled. "We have to dress and go downstairs. The Gleasons now we're here now. They'll be waiting for us."

"Well, we're already fashionably late, remember?" The bed, the sparkle in her eyes, the rosy pout of her mouth, all of it combined to make him hard as hell. "An appetizer, Taryn, that's all."

Her dark lashes dipped, covering her eyes as she walked to him. "What sort of appetizer did you have in mind, Coop?"

Lightly cupping her shoulders, Coop pressed her into the soft mattress, then straddled her body, careful not to crush her with his weight. To hell with it, they were already late, what was a few more minutes? He had more immediate matters to attend to. Like her mouth.

"I'm going to kiss you, Taryn."

Her body jerked and her eyes dropped to his lips. "Yes," she sighed. "Do it."

He lowered his head, brushing his mouth over hers lightly, pulling back, dipping, kissing her again. Her sweet taste went straight to his head.

Both of them.

When her hands wrapped around his

shoulders and pulled him down, he groaned and deepened the kiss, spearing into her mouth with a need that bordered on desperation. Rimming the inside of her lips and cheeks, he found and stroked her tongue, demanding more from her. Accepting it when she gave it.

Coop grasped her face between his hands and delved further into her welcoming mouth. Again and again their tongues met, slid wetly together, retreated.

His hand coursed down her neck, over the thundering pulse beating at the base of her throat, flicking open the buttons of her silky, shimmery shirt. When his fingers found the bare, burning skin of her stomach, he groaned again, lifting his mouth from hers to look down at her.

A small silver and amethyst cat dangled over her belly button and he sucked in a breath, touching it with his finger, making it sway, making her buck.

"Damn, that's sexy," he told her. His eyes left the belly piercing to travel up her ribcage to her voluptuous breasts which spilled over the top of her cream-colored bra, inviting mounds of soft flesh he simply had to touch. To taste.

Peeling the shirt all the way apart, he shifted again, inching down her body. He looked at Taryn. Her eyes were closed and her bottom lip was firmly caught between her teeth. Her hands curled with tight pressure over his shoulders.

Coop trailed his fingers along the sides of her small waist, up her ribcage, over the sides of her bra, finally settling his palms over the tops of her breasts. She moaned, back arching.

"Open your eyes, Taryn," he said.

Her dark black lashes lifted slowly.

He fingered the heated metal binding holding the cups of her bra together. "Do you know how much I want to undo this clasp? How much I want to take your bra off and look at you?"

She smiled wickedly and lifted her pelvis, bumping his hard arousal. "I can take a guess." Taryn licked her lips, her hands falling away from his shoulders to the mattress beside her head. "So, do it, Coop."

With one deft twist of his fingers, Coop undid the clasp. Sitting up on the mattress beside her, he moved the bra away, baring her. *Incredible.* She was everything he knew she'd be. Soft, pliant and arousing.

He felt the shiver that wracked her and met her gaze. Placing his hands on her wrists, he dropped a soft kiss on her lips. "Don't move, okay? Just give me a minute."

She nodded.

Releasing her, he again swept his fingers down her neck, around her breasts until he circled her deep-red, hard nipples. She gasped when he grazed his thumb over them. Coop leaned down and closed his mouth over one, strumming his tongue over the stiff bud.

Her hands tangled in his hair. Coop switched his attention to her other nipple and she bucked.

"Coop," she murmured. "Yes. I like that."

So did he, but he drew back with a regretful sigh. Tugging the edges of her shirt over her bare, beautiful breasts, he kissed her softly.

"Coop, what's wrong?" She sat up and the shirt parted, tempting him to return.

He stood instead, raking his hair and grinning ruefully. "Cocktails. Damn it."

Offering her a hand up, he tugged her against him, caressing the slope of her hip. "I don't want to rush anything with you, Taryn."

Her smoky, passion-infused eyes nearly had him taking her back down to the bed.

"Don't worry, Tiger, we've got all night."

She winked and trailed her fingertips down his chest, hovering at the waistband of his slacks. He inhaled sharply, covering her hand with his. She laughed as she sauntered to the bathroom.

Turning, she leaned on the doorjamb. "I'll just freshen up my makeup, unless," her brow raised over twinkling eyes. "You need to take a cold shower."

"Brat," he said, reaching for the buttons of his shirt. "Go on, I know it takes women forever to get ready."

She licked her lips and he felt her gaze against every inch of his chest as the shirt opened. "Oh, I'm ready."

"Taryn." Her name came out in a warning growl.

"Okay, okay." The door closed on her sultry laugh.

Taryn sipped her after-dinner drink, listening

with amused interest as the woman in front of her related a story involving her tiny dog, an exclusive salon and a rodent-fearing stylist.

"Pip was scared to pieces," declared the diamond-wearing matron. A small scowl twisted her brows. "I had the manager nearly in tears as I gave him the lecture of a lifetime. Of course I swore I'd never go back."

"But...?" Taryn prompted.

She grinned and winked. "Who could resist free manicures for the rest of the year?"

The small group laughed, including Taryn. She lifted her glass in tribute. "A very wise woman."

"Thank you, dear, I thought it was rather brilliant myself."

"What was, Estelle?" Monica Gleason insinuated herself into the small circle, conveniently right at Taryn's side.

She steeled herself, waiting for the pounce she knew was coming.

"My manicure story, Monica."

"Ah, yes." She turned her shoulder toward Pip's owner, neatly cutting her off. "Miss Kirkpatrick, are you enjoying yourself?"

Taryn pondered the question, looking for hidden acidity, surprised to find none. She offered her hostess a smile. "Yes, Mrs. Gleason, thank you. Please, call me Taryn. You have a beautiful home."

Monica trilled and waved a hand negligently. "It's been in the family for generations, but it is much too far in the country for my tastes. I prefer the sophisticated comforts of the city."

Taryn tensed, sensing the claws were about to be unsheathed. "Each has its unique offerings," she said neutrally.

"Quite." Monica studied her for a moment before stepping back and facing the others still crowding around. "Did Miss Kirkpatrick tell you what she does for a living?"

Ah, there's the acid.

Pip's owner, bless her heart, beamed excitedly. "Oh yes, Monica. How fun!" She giggled and winked at Taryn. "Can you just imagine fitting all those lovely men in their costumes?"

Monica's lips tightened, but Taryn doubted the others noticed.

"One wonders how Cooper feels about that."

Her patently false smile grated on Taryn's dwindling nerves.

"He doesn't mind, Mrs. Gleason. He knows it's just a part of my job." If the hostess could be false, it was only polite to follow her lead and lie out of both sides of her mouth, wasn't it? Taryn had no idea how Coop would feel about it, not that it mattered. Now, more than ever, she was determined to keep this soon-to-be affair light and fun, all sex and definitely no substance.

"That is all well and good, but don't you have any ambition?"

Taryn sipped at her wine again, trying to temper her tongue. This was not her past, it was Coop's future. "I am content, Mrs. Gleason. Happy with what I do."

The back of her neck tingled and Taryn

turned her head just as Coop arrived, his hand sliding comfortingly along her back. "Good evening, ladies. You are all looking very lovely this evening."

The group at large tittered, easily charmed by his smooth words. Monica preened most of all. Latching onto his arm, she tugged him a bit closer.

"Cooper, have you met everyone?"

His palm stayed firmly splayed on Taryn's back, a warm reminder that she wasn't alone.

"No, I'm positive I haven't." He winked at the four women. "I would have remembered such beauty."

Taryn groaned and rolled her eyes. "He's the one who should be on stage, don't you think?"

The women laughed, relaxed sounds of true amusement.

Again, Monica's mouth twisted and pulled into nearly a pout before she pasted a smile on and made the introductions.

Taryn stood silently by his side, listening to him effortlessly win over the women with his quick wit. One by one, their husbands arrived, more introductions ensued and she was astounded by the ease with which he deftly steered the conversation to focus on them and their accomplishments.

If she didn't know better, she'd swear he was a politician. The thought soured her stomach and took her breath as memories rolled over her. The air around her took on a heaviness that settled on her chest and she wiggled under Coop's hand.

"Please, excuse me, I'll be back shortly." Not waiting for anyone's permission to leave, she spun and walked away as gracefully as she could. Visions of Cinderella's sprint from the ball flitted through her mind, but instead of making her smile, tonight she could empathize with the need to escape.

Escape her past, her memories, who she'd once turned herself into.

The veranda was long, wide and blessedly unoccupied. Sinking down onto an ornately carved cast-stone bench, Taryn stared into the moonlight reflected in the koi pond just beyond the stairs.

Yes, she could meld into this lifestyle. Knew all the words to say, the right times to laugh, when to stroke an ego and when to be deferential.

But deferential was not who she was anymore. *Never again.* She could do it, but she sure as hell didn't want to.

Closing her eyes tightly, she dragged deep bursts full of honeysuckle-tinted air into her lungs, batting away the panic threatening. What was done was done. The past couldn't hurt her anymore. She would not allow Monica Gleason the same power she'd once given her ex-husband and his circle of politically-driven cronies.

Not even for a weekend of what promised to be mind-blowing, among other things, sex.

"Taryn?"

Coop's deep voice stroked over her skin and she shivered, weakening briefly. Maybe not.

She shook her head. No, damn it, definitely not.

"I think I should go home."

"What? Why?" He sat next to her, thigh pressing hers, shoulders rubbing. If she but leaned forward the slightest bit, his arm would brush her breasts. She was so aware of him, her nipples sprang to life immediately.

"I thought I could do this, Coop. Thought I could waltz in here like I've done so many times before and let it roll off my back. Her opinion of me shouldn't matter."

"Whose opinion?"

She started, realizing he really had no clue who she was talking about. The man was alarmingly astute. Not noticing made no sense to her. She glared at him. "Monica's, of course."

He nodded. "Yeah, that's what I figured." He steepled his fingers and tapped them against his chin. "I have to tell you, I've heard nothing but praise for you, Taryn. You've enthralled every one of us."

Another zing sparked through her. "Even you?"

"Especially me. Does her opinion matter?"

She scowled. "No. Yes. No. Damn it, Coop." Kicking at a leaf that dared litter the veranda, she sighed gustily. "It matters only in that it doesn't reflect badly on you and from that to Mr. Gleason. I told you I wouldn't lose you this deal and I meant it. That's why I ought to leave. I'm not very good at kow-towing."

"Honey," he said very gently. "is anyone asking you to?"

She stilled. "Well, no, I suppose not."

He chuckled, wrapping his arm around her shoulders and squeezing briefly. "Be yourself, Taryn. Those who can't accept who you are and what you do aren't worth the breath it would take to convince them you're a gem."

"Does that include Monica?"

Coop was silent for so long the night sounds of crickets and gently splashing water seemed abnormally loud. "I'm not asking you to compromise yourself, Taryn," he finally answered.

"That's not an answer."

"No, it's not, but it's all I have." He stood. "Listen, the band has started playing. Dance with me. Please?"

She slowly rose, appraising him in the luminous glow of the nearly full moon and the golden light spilling from the ballroom. "I'll stay, Coop and I'll do my best to be civil, but you should know the yes-woman I used to be is long gone."

He raised a brow, and she could see she'd surprised him with her description of her past self. Oh, the stories she could tell him. She didn't need to walk an inch in Monica's high-heels she knew exactly what it was like. Years of being enveloped, smothered, stifled did that to a woman who trusted and loved the wrong man. "You? A yes-woman? I find that very hard to believe." He held out his arms. "Dance with me."

She hung back. "Coop, I don't know."

"It's easy." He gently pulled again, lowering his cheek to hers, brushing a kiss on her lips.

"Come on, I want to hold you in my arms."

Taryn's breasts swelled at his huskily whispered words, the strong hand at her back, the rough scrape of his five o'clock shadow. She wanted him to hold her, too. But upstairs. Naked, him wanting her as fiercely as she did him. She could still feel the slick heat of his tongue wrapped around her nipple, the gentle touch of his fingers caressing her body. Briefly, she considered trying to coerce him back to the privacy of their room, but knew she shouldn't. He needed to remain a while and make a good impression. They had the rest of the night for sex. She grinned. However, a little more of a preview couldn't hurt. "All right, but keep it slow."

His lips quirked up as he eased her onto the floor and into the rhythm of the music. "I told you, I plan on taking my time."

Coop held her lightly but with firm pressure, steering her deftly through the waltzing crowd. Taryn tried to concentrate on the steps, but kept losing count whenever he squeezed her waist or stroked her hip. Which seemed to be often.

"Coop, you're not making this any easier."

He chuckled, pulling her closer, until her nipples brushed his chest. Even through her Chanel dress she responded to him. Instantly throbbing, Taryn once again was all for ditching the rest of the dancing and going back to their room. Having become accustomed to heeding her own whims over the years, she decided not to fight it any longer.

She wanted him. Looking up, she sucked in a

deep breath. Passion burned hotly from his eyes, darkening them to an intense, emerald color. Just as she pictured him so often in her dreams. "Coop," she whispered. "I hear our room calling."

His nostrils flared, fingers constricting at her waist. "Despite the way it looks, I didn't bring you here to start an affair, Taryn."

Sliding her palm down his chest to the zipper of his slacks, she toyed with the silver tab. "You want me, Coop." She applied more pressure and he groaned as he trapped her wrist.

"Hell, yeah, I want you, Taryn. But—"

"No buts. Make love with me."

Indecision warred in his eyes before he lifted his head, staring into the brightly lit ballroom. Taryn squeezed his hard cock and he bucked. His mouth crashed down on hers and he ripped her hand away.

His kiss burned and consumed her, made her forget they stood on the veranda in plain sight. She could only think about absorbing him, any way she could. Taryn tugged at the buttons of his shirt, desperate to feel the crisp hair she knew covered his muscular chest.

Coop broke the kiss. "Are you sure this is what you want? Here?"

Through the fog of her urgent desire, Taryn managed a shaky grin. "Oh, yeah, Cooper Malone, you have no idea how long I've dreamed of this."

Chapter Five

"I should shave," Coop said, rubbing his bristly jaw. He was chagrined to find his hand shook. Hell, his whole body vibrated like he'd stuck his finger in a light socket. He couldn't remember ever being this aware of a woman. This nervous. This excited.

Taryn leaned against the locked bedroom door and gave him a slow, inviting smile. "Don't shave on my account, Coop." She winked. "I like the way your beard feels on my skin."

Her words threatened the thin veneer of control he'd maintained all the way up the stairs.

"Yeah?"

With slow, measured steps, Coop closed the distance between them, crowding her against the door. Bracing his hands on either side of her head, he searched her ice-blue eyes for hesitation or indecision. Because he knew, once he started ravishing her, he wouldn't be able to stop. "You're sure, Taryn? This is what you want?"

She parted his tuxedo jacket, wrapping her fingers around his waist. "I'm very sure. I want you, Cooper Malone. And I intend to have you."

"Brazen little thing, aren't you?"

Her sultry laugh shot straight to his cock.

"Oh yeah, when I want something bad enough."

"Unbutton my shirt," he said softly.

She tugged the material from the back of his pants, fingers dipping beneath his waistband for a quick feel. He growled in warning and she chuckled again.

"I can't help it. I've been eyeing these buns for weeks. Just had to see if they felt as good as they look."

"And?" he asked warily.

"Well, your briefs are made of cotton. I'll let you know about your butt when I get you out of them."

It was his turn to laugh. "I'll show you mine if you show me yours."

"Deal. And since you've already seen me, let's start with you." Nimbly she undid his small pearl buttons, neck to navel. Her rapid motion slowed as she moved to the ones hanging level with his crotch.

Coop gritted his teeth each time the backs of her fingers grazed his hard, aching cock. Deliberately, he was sure. Time to regain some control.

Stepping away, he shucked his jacket, tossing it toward a chair. Flipping open his cuff links, he stuck them in his pocket and peeled his shirt from his shoulders, heaving it at the chair, as well. He looked at her, hiding a smile at her openly hungry stare.

"Your turn, Taryn."

Her filmy pink gown, sleeveless and sporting a surprisingly modest cut in the front, was made of two parts. The bottom of the bodice was bordered in delicate beads a shade darker than the fuller skirt it topped.

She pushed away from the door, hands lifting to her nape. Her head dipped down as she struggled with the fastening.

"Need some help?"

"Yes, please."

Turning her back to him, she held her wavy blond hair out of the way. He unhooked the wire clasp and slid the zipper down the lean length of her back, savoring each bit of her golden flesh. As the silky material parted, he discovered she wasn't wearing a bra.

"There," he rasped, forcing his hands away. Slow and easy. Damn near impossible when all he wanted was to take her fast and hard. "Turn around, Taryn."

She swung around, hands cupping her breasts, holding the bodice in place. That wicked, come-hither smile teased her mouth again. "Shall I drop it, Coop?"

"Yes. I want to see you."

"And then?" She sauntered forward, the pink material inching down with each step, baring more of her creamy flesh. When she reached him, she let go.

She stood before him, shoulders back and

full breasts millimeters away from his skin. One deep breath from either of them and her nipples would scrape through the hair matting his chest. Though entranced by the vision she so sweetly presented, Coop caught a dart of apprehension zing through her eyes. *Taryn, nervous?* The vixen who seduced him without even trying, was uncertain?

The knowledge cut the edge of his hunger, gentled his touch. He cupped her shoulders, rubbing her silky skin with his thumbs. Lowering his head, he kissed her with soft pressure, sweeping his tongue along the edge of her full bottom lip. The slight tension seeped from her and her arms came up, circling his neck, flattening her breasts to his chest.

They both gasped at the contact.

Wild, burning, relentless. Taryn had to relieve this need. Douse the burning and throbbing that rushed from her breasts to settle between her legs. Clenching her thighs tightly together didn't give her the relief she needed. She moaned into Coop's hot mouth, brushing her nipples over his hair-roughened chest. Taryn pulled away from his demanding kiss, gritting her teeth at the riot of sensation beating at her. No dream lover could compete with the live heat of Coop's mouth, no matter how good.

Her pussy throbbed and pulsed with increasing desire. Each time his lips teased her nipples, she climbed a little closer to orgasm. *Unbelievable.* That had never happened to her before just from having her breasts touched. "Coop," she whispered, pressing her forehead to his shoulder, seeking any bit of calmness. His hot scent—male, musk, and sex—rolled and wrapped around her. More intoxicating than any wine, she drew in a lungful, savoring it.

He suckled at her neck, trailing open-mouthed kisses along her skin. Again, she squeezed her thighs, shuddering at the quick pulse zinging along her clit. She wanted to feel him everywhere, touching her, tasting her, loving her until she could take no more.

Tangling her fingers in his hair, she tugged his mouth back to hers, thrusting her tongue forward, finding his. Openly demanding, she ground her hips to his, moaning into his champagne-flavored kiss at his stiffness.

Tearing away, Coop fell back a few steps. "Take it all off, Taryn."

She licked her lips, tasting him and quickly found the zipper at her waist. Despite the fumbling, shaking grip of her fingers, she managed to slide it down, shoving the expensive, frothy gown to the floor.

His deep inhalation, the dark, hazy passion of his green-eyed stare and the insistent erection in his tuxedo pants held her in place, allowing him to look his fill. She'd worn her white lace, barely-there panties tonight just for this reason.

His appreciative groan was well worth the decision. The white triangle of peek-a-boo lace barely concealed her true blond curls, but they showed enough to keep him wild.

What would he say when he saw her fully?

"Your turn," she murmured huskily.

Nearly as quickly as she'd disrobed, Coop's

pants hit the floor.

"Oh, my," she breathed softly, eyes fastened to the long, hard cock pushing against his dark-gray boxer briefs.

"Why don't you take a closer look?" he suggested.

Her body had never felt so tense and ready. Walking the short distance to him caused a delicious crescendo of friction between her thighs and she knew the crotch of her panties was soaked.

He cupped her breasts, his hands warm and strong on her flesh and Taryn's eyes fluttered down as she leaned into him. Coop's hands stilled.

"No, watch me."

She did, shuddering when he caught one nipple in his thumb and forefinger. Reality and dream blurred and blended as she saw him do to her what she had so often fantasized. But his touch was so much surer, so much better than in her dreams.

When he switched nipples, Taryn flattened her palms to his chest, clenching her fingers in his mass of dark masculine hair, enjoying his sharp hiss.

That she could rouse such a reaction thrilled her and she trailed her hands downward, pushing his arms aside and found the elastic waistband of his briefs.

"Time for the unwrapping," she murmured, sinking to her knees in front of him.

Coop's feet slid apart and he crossed his arms over his chest. Despite his look of calm,

Taryn saw the rapid beat of his pulse at his throat, the tightly clenched muscles ticking in his jaw.

Carefully she eased the material out and away, letting it fall through nerveless fingers as his cock was revealed. "Beautiful," she whispered, licking her lips.

"Christ, Taryn, don't do that." His voice held a rough note of teetering control. Her gaze met his hooded eyes briefly. His green eyes burned and sparked, his nostrils flared and his sensual lips were pressed into a tight line.

She dropped her stare back down, mesmerized by the long, well-built strength of his penis. Long and heavy with his desire for her, the tip glistened with further proof of his need. She wanted to feel him.

The intensity and frequency of her dream liaisons with him gave her a strange sense of familiarity. Would he like her mouth on his cock as much in real life as he did in those midnight fantasies? Only one way to find out.

Taryn eased forward, closing her eyes as she slid her mouth over the flared head of his dick.

"Jesus," he said with a gasp, hands tangling in her hair. "Like that."

With a long, slow motion she pulled back, trailing her tongue along the throbbing underside of his cock, flicking at the sharply rounded head before sinking back down as far as she could. Over and over she stroked him, savoring the saltiness of his building excitement with each motion.

A guttural grunt escaped him and he pulled

hard on her hair, stilling her. "No more."

Taryn inhaled deeply, pulling his spicy masculine scent into her nose. With one last strong draw, she reluctantly released him, grinning at the faint pop as his head withdrew.

Coop shuddered as he moved out of the reach of her talented mouth. One more lash of her tongue and she'd have him coming. Not how he wanted to start the night. He tugged her to her feet and into a hug designed more to buy him time to regain his control.

The effect of her soft, full breasts flattened against his chest did nothing to help. Neither did the scent of her arousal mingling with her musky perfume. Without loosening his hold, Coop moved backward until his knees hit the edge of the bed.

"I hope you had enough sleep last night, Miss Kirkpatrick." He sat down, standing her between his spread knees.

"Yeah? Why's that?"

He traced the thin band of her panties, her abdomen spasming beneath his fingertip. Replacing it with his mouth, he nipped at her resilient flesh, diving beneath her silver jewelry to swipe at the hollow of her belly button, absorbing the small tremors. "I plan on learning every inch of your body, in close detail. And a masterpiece like this takes time."

She giggled and pushed at his shoulders. Snagging her around the waist, he let his momentum take them down to the bed. Her wild curls spilled around them, creating a curtain enclosing their faces.

Coop lifted his head and kissed her lightly, before twisting her off his body and to the soft comforter, flat on her back.

Her smile slipped a bit as she covered her breasts, pushing them to the center of her chest.

"Don't," he murmured, moving her hand. "You're beautiful. Natural."

"They're too big."

"Good Lord, woman, they're perfect. Soft, real, all you. And look how sensitive you are." He licked her nipple, drawing the tip to a tighter, harder point. "See?" he whispered. "So sweet."

"You don't mind?"

He lifted his head and stared at her, surprised by the sudden hesitancy. For all her bravado and sexual innuendo, it was clear she didn't consider her breasts her best asset. He wondered why.

"Honey, if I didn't think I'd shoot like a bottle rocket, I'd show you just how much I don't mind." Pressing a long, wet kiss to her flesh, he moved up to her ear. "I'd slide between them until we both came."

Her eyes lit up and she licked her lips. He really wished she'd quit doing that. With a wicked smile, she reached for him. "Why not?"

He trapped her hand. "No way, lady, it's my turn."

Hooking his thumbs under the tiny strap of her underwear, he started to peel them away.

"Wait," she gasped.

Coop raised a brow in question, but stopped. "Problem?"

She blushed. A rosy hue that started between

her luscious breasts and worked its way up to her cheeks. "Um, more like an eccentricity."

"Really?" he drawled, even more intrigued. He drummed his fingers on her hipbones. "What kind?"

She cleared her throat, covering her eyes with both hands. "I can't say. Just promise not to laugh."

He grinned, but only because she couldn't see him. "Okay, no laughing."

"Take my panties off, Coop."

Amused, fascinated and horny as hell, he peeled the white fabric away from her toned, taut body. The first thing he noticed was that she was a true blond. The second was the neatly trimmed happy face grinning at him.

He traced the design with his forefinger. Her hair was downy soft, another oddity.

"Well, say something, dammit," she muttered, eyes still hidden.

"You shave by stencil?"

Her chest heaved and her lips parted on a wide smile. She propped up on her elbows. "Very funny."

"Nah, I think it's cute." He petted the blond design. "And soft."

"Condi—" her voice hitched when he dipped lower, "—conditioner."

God, she was wet. All semblance of teasing fell away as he parted her lips. Her butt lifted and she dropped to the bed again.

"Open up for me, Taryn."

She did, spreading her supple legs, drawing her knees up a bit. Deep red and beckoning, the picture of her so wantonly displayed for him had his cock twitching.

Cupping her pussy, he ground his palm along her slick clitoris while slipping a finger into her. She jerked, mumbling incoherently.

Hot and tight, she was all the things fantasies were made of. Especially his. He pulled out, dipped in again and again, driving her to the brink just as she had him.

"Coop, please, I need you inside me."

"Not yet, Taryn," he whispered, quickening his motion and her hips bucked violently. "Come for me."

Her breath whistled out as her legs flattened on the bed, hips rising to meet his fingers. "Not fair," she managed.

"No," he agreed as he leaned forward, found her clit and engulfed it with his mouth.

Her screech as she orgasmed was quickly muffled by the pillow she slammed over her face. Coop stiffened his tongue, dragging it along her honey-slick labia while she trembled and murmured a faint litany of "Oh, my God."

The pillow flew to the side of the mattress and he lifted his head, slowly slipping his finger free.

"Dammit, Coop."

But her feline smile of satisfaction belied any heat from her words.

"Just taking the edge off."

Her eyes glinted before dropping to his still throbbing cock. "Looks like your edge is a bit needy, too."

He nodded as he rose.

"What are you doing?"

Striding across the room, he rummaged through his shaving bag, grabbing a strip of condoms he'd packed. Just in case.

Taryn's lithe body writhed sinuously as she stretched on the bed and he ripped a packet open hastily, sheathing himself in less time than it took to blink.

Approaching the bed, he grabbed her ankles and tugged her to the edge. She laughed, clutching at his forearms.

"My, how horny you are."

"Yes," he murmured, kissing her mouth. "And since you're the cause, you ought to fix it, don't you think?"

"Definitely."

Her hand found his covered erection and guided him down, fitting his head to the slick opening between her lower lips. Hooking his thumbs under her butt, he tilted her up and sank in.

"Oh, yeah. God, Taryn."

"Damn, you feel good." She mewled and twisted, fingernails biting into his arms. "Fuck me, Coop."

Her words made his heat-encased cock surge. He felt the sweat at the base of his spine with the effort it took to go slow and easy. Her body clamped around him with snug precision and each time he withdrew, she sucked him back in.

When her muscles contracted, squeezing him, he jerked. "Christ, Taryn, don't. I can't—"

She cupped his jaw, ice-blue eyes burning with the same fever rushing through him. "Fast and hard, Coop, you promised."

He groaned, bowing his head, nuzzling the passion-slickened hollow of her neck and surged forward, fingers digging into the softness of her ass. She met him all the way, tilting her pelvis up with each thrust.

Coop knew he was about to come, couldn't control it any longer, she just felt too good, too tight. So damn tight. Gritting his teeth, he shifted so that each thrust brought him in contact with her clit.

Taryn's hands clutched at his waist, drawing him in deeper and harder until she emitted a muffled cry. Her body tightened around him, milking him unmercifully and Coop slammed into her welcoming body one last time, shuddering at the depth of his release.

Dropping his head to her shoulder, he tried to catch his breath, and his runaway control, neither of which cooperated. Beneath him, Taryn continued to tremble, her teeth firmly entrenched in bottom lip, her eyes squeezed tightly shut.

"Taryn?"

She shook her head, but she relaxed her mouth enough to smile. "Just a sec," she wheezed.

"Shh," he murmured, slipping from her body.

She gasped and jerked strongly, one hand flying to her mouth as her head thrashed on the bunched up sheets, the other cupped over her pussy.

Coop rubbed small circles into her abdomen, lightly caressing her warm flesh until her shivering stopped.

Finally, her eyes opened and she offered him a hazy, drowsy smile. "Sorry," she murmured, covering his hand with hers. "Aftershocks."

He grinned back, arrogantly pleased by her reaction. Leaning down, he gently kissed her mouth, laving her red, swollen bottom lip with his tongue. "Wanna do it again?"

Her fingers tightened on his. "You up to it?"

He grimaced, aware of a sudden discomfort. "Uh, no, actually. Not yet. Give me a few minutes."

With a small yawn, she nodded, snuggling into his chest, tangling her nails in his hair. "'kay."

Coop didn't have the heart to move, so he gritted his teeth, shifted his hips and slid his hand up and down her satin smooth back. She relaxed and in no time he caught the slow, rhythmic breathing that assured him she was asleep.

Sliding from the bed, Coop made his way to the bathroom and cleaned up, still a bit awed by the speed and incredible passion of it all.

He hadn't brought her here to make love to her, despite his roll of condoms. A guy could hope, but his situation with the Gleasons was so tentative, he hadn't really put much stock in the idea of making love with Taryn. Not here.

But he had. Like a fool, he'd rushed things. It wasn't how he'd meant their first time to be. But she seemed able to throw him off-kilter with ease. Destroy all his organized plans and send him into another orbit altogether. Not something he was accustomed to.

He grimaced then bent to splash water on his face, before padding barefoot and naked back to the bedroom. The cool, rational voice in the back of his head urged caution, warned him she was a hazard. But to what, he wasn't sure. Taryn Kirkpatrick presented a tantalizing and confusing set of contradictions. A woman who exuded sex, fun and fantasy but who also morphed with chameleon-like ability into the perfect social elitist.

Coop tugged on a brand new pair of pajama bottoms—stiff and uncomfortable as hell— and walked to the bed, staring down at her. Idiotic as it sounded, she looked like an angel with her pink lips slightly parted and her golden curls falling around her shoulders.

In his world, angels were frequently trod upon but he got the feeling she would be more than able to take care of herself. A notion that worried him. Taryn's eclectic personality, well, from what scant information and impressions he had of her, did not lend itself to taking condescension quietly. And the barest misplaced word could ruin what he'd worked weeks over.

She shifted and sighed. Coop shook himself, trying to pull his head out of his ass, all the while reminding himself she'd done absolutely nothing to warrant his censure. And despite the possibilities, he found on closer inspection he did not regret starting this affair, even if it was done under Monica Gleason's gleaming, expensive roof.

Coop tugged the blanket and sheet Taryn

slept on and she mumbled, sat up then scooted under them, rolling to her side, never really waking up. He crawled in beside her, lying flat on his back.

What was he going to do?

He'd never indulged in a one-night stand in his life. Never slept with a woman he knew virtually nothing about. His previous relationships had all been planned, plotted and predictable. Carefully evaluated and even more carefully ended. Nothing like the passionate, near-uncontrollable lust he'd experienced since meeting Taryn.

But she didn't belong in his world. Despite mouthing all the correct phrases, smiling at all the right times and dressing perfectly for the part. It was the haunted, hollow look in her eyes on the veranda that made him question the sanity of his decision to indulge both of their impulses.

With a stretch and long, low *mmm*, Taryn rolled over, feeling the delicious twinges and aches of a well-loved body. Immediately aware of Coop's big body next to her, she shifted to her side and propped her head on her palm, staring at his face.

The bright August moon shone in from the floor to ceiling window, bathing his strong jaw and broad shoulders in silvery light.

Reaching out, she drew her fingertip over his bottom lip. He nipped at her, turning his head and meeting her eyes.

The expression in them stilled her questing hand that had just dipped beneath the sheet.

"Coop? Are you okay?"

The silence filled with tension in a ridiculously short amount of time and Taryn mentally cringed. *Here it comes*. Looking away from him, she sat up, holding the sheet to her chest, desperately searching the dark room for her clothes.

"Damn, damn, damn," she mumbled, scooting to the far side of the bed and swinging her feet to the floor. "When will I learn?"

Strong hands circled her waist, halting her flight. She closed her eyes, heart and body tensed in anticipation and a lingering sense of uncertainty.

"Going somewhere?"

She cast him a look over her shoulder. "Having second thoughts?"

The bed dipped and the sheet fell as he whipped it off. His lips pressed warmly to her throat, his hands coming around to cup her breasts.

She cursed her own weakness even as she leaned against his fur-covered chest.

"Just thinking, Taryn," he murmured, dark voice as seductive as the fingers toying with her nipples. "This is as new to me as it is to you. A lot to absorb."

"Yes," she hissed, both in agreement and a plea for him to continue rolling her nipples.

"Why don't we take it one day at a time?"

More tension drained from her at his words— exactly what she was looking for. No strings for this part-time affair.

"Sounds like, oh—" She spread her legs

when his palm slid down her stomach, affording him better access. "Sounds like a television show."

Coop's chuckle traveled up the sensitive flesh of her hip.

"Lift up," he said.

She looked up at him, brow quirked at the sudden force in his tone.

"Why?"

"Ah, ah, no questions, woman, just do it."

Her mouth went dry even as her pussy grew wetter with his words. Heart picking up a rapid pace, she slowly pulled away and lifted up. The bed moved again and suddenly he surrounded her totally from beneath, his legs on either side of hers, arms cradling her, rigid cock thrusting strongly at the small of her back.

He nipped at her neck, hands drifting over her body.

God, she wanted him to touch her everywhere, all at the same time. The burn he seemed to so easily ignite in her threatened to melt all her good sense. One day at a time? Hell, she'd be lucky to make it through one night without combusting.

"Taryn?"

"Hmm?"

His big palms found the insides of her thighs and pulled gently until her legs splayed widely over his.

"Minute's up."

She heard him rip open the packet and grinned. "Thank God."

His hands slipped between her thighs, lifting

her up even more. "Move forward a little," he whispered, voice sensually rough. Demanding.

She did, fingertips grasping at the edges of the bed. Only when she looked back over her shoulder did she realize just how open she'd made herself to him. The idea excited her. "Coop," she groaned.

"I know, Taryn." His fingers cupped her butt, tilting her up ever so slightly and she trembled, afraid to fall, more afraid he wouldn't continue.

But he did and they both gasped as he slid easily into her wetness.

She'd never made love at this angle and it was a feeling of fullness, of newness. Guided by the strength in his hands, Taryn rotated her hips.

Beneath her, his thighs bunched and rippled as he began to thrust. She dropped her head back to his shoulder, eyes closed, hands now fisted tightly at her side.

"Touch yourself, Taryn."

"What?"

One hand left her hip and uncurled her fingers, sliding her palm over her own stomach and down to their joined bodies.

"Touch yourself."

"No, I couldn't—"

"Together?"

Their joined fingers hovered above her clitoris, which surged forward with each slow thrust Coop made into her. Taryn swallowed hard, knowing she wanted it. Wanted him. He couldn't know how often she'd dreamed of him, only to awaken with her body in a fevered state of orgasm and her hands in her panties.

With trembling fingers, she stroked her clit, breathing harshly at the instant lustful gratification.

Coop's mouth did erotic, incredible things to her neck while their fingers and his strong, potent thrusts pushed her desire ever higher.

She could almost believe she was back in her dream world, making love with him, doing things she'd never dared to do before. He set her truly free.

Her hand moved faster, hips jerking wildly. Coop clutched her waist again, pulling her down to meet his upstroke.

When he groaned and swelled within her, then slammed hard and stilled, she flicked her clit again, seeking the same release.

"Taryn, Taryn, let me."

His fingers moved hers aside, taking over the job. She was so ready, it only took him a few circular motions and she stiffened, riding the orgasm, and the cock still embedded within her, to completion.

The tremors lasted much longer this time and when she finally rose, it was to find her legs shaky. Stumbling to the bathroom, she flipped on the light. Turning to look at him, she giggled at the way he'd flopped back on the bed. He raised his head.

"Yes?" he asked with tired amusement.

"I could get to like this affair of convenience."

Chapter Six

Affair of convenience. For the remainder of the weekend, the words grated on Coop like fresh parmesan at an Italian restaurant. Settling a hip on the white-washed concrete fence surrounding the veranda, Coop watched Taryn charm an old judge, his polar opposite young wife and Troy Gleason as they sipped after-brunch cocktails. It was the last hurrah before everyone returned to the city. One final opportunity for him to cement the contacts he'd made. But Coop found he couldn't budge.

He had to admit the weekend had turned out to be one full of surprises, the biggest of which was Taryn. She'd wowed them all. Almost all, he acknowledged with a grimace. Taryn's seemingly effortless integration into her social circle did not sit well with Monica. Though not totally obvious in her irritation, she'd managed several pointed comments designed to pull Taryn down.

To his date's credit, she didn't respond in an equally catty fashion. At least, not in public. He grinned. Taryn let loose her frustration when they went to bed. God, she was amazing. He'd never had another sexual partner like her. And he'd never known another woman like her, either.

"She's a gem, that one, Malone," a raspy voice informed him.

Coop looked at Thomas Locke and nodded. "Yes, sir, she is." He tensed, waiting. The man's reputation, both personal and business, rivaled the ferocity of a great white. Though they shared the same drive to succeed, Coop knew this man was not above cutthroat tactics to get what he wanted. Locke, for all his high-profile business acumen, was not a contact Coop worked too hard to cultivate.

"Smart girl, listens, sees right through the bullshit, but goes along with it anyway. Yep, she's a good one."

The man ambled away, stopping by the table to shake hands and make his goodbyes. Taryn offered her hand, but he hauled her to her feet and wrapped her in a bear hug.

Coop smothered a smile as her wide-eyed gaze caught his, clearly signaling help. He stood and walked over as Locke released her.

"Taryn, you about ready to go?"

"Yes," she said emphatically, relief loud in the small word. Clearing her throat she wiggled her shoulders and turned to the group at the table. "It's been a lovely weekend, Mr. Gleason, please thank your wife for inviting me."

Troy nodded slightly. "Of course, Miss Kirkpatrick."

"Judge Carter, Mrs. Carter, it was a pleasure meeting both of you."

The young Mrs. Carter stood and hurried around the table, taking both of Taryn's hands in hers. "You won't forget to find out about the tour, will you? The kids would love to see the workings of a real production."

"I'll talk with my stage manager about it tomorrow, but it shouldn't be a problem. I'll call you as soon as I hear.

"Wonderful." Mrs. Carter looked at him. "We'll see you again, Mr. Malone. My husband has your number, correct?"

"Yes ma'am."

"Good. You'll be hearing from me."

Coop nodded and slid Taryn's hands from the other woman's.

"Troy, we're all set for Wednesday at ten."

"We'll be there, Cooper." Troy shook his hand and waved them off. "Go on, it's getting late and I'm sure you two don't want to be trapped in a car all day." He winked.

Hell, no. Coop tightened his fingers on Taryn's and tugged her forward. "Right."

They walked along the carefully laid out meandering garden path that led around to the front of the house. Brent stood at the entryway and waved to them.

"Got your bags right here, Miss Taryn. Mr. Malone, I'll have your car pulled 'round."

"Thank you, Brent, appreciate that," Coop said. The man beamed and hurried away.

"You remembered his name," Taryn murmured.

He frowned at her. "You sound surprised."

"I guess I am a bit. Most guys I know—knew—wouldn't have remembered his name if it'd been tattooed on his forehead."

His gut tightened a bit. "I'm not most guys, Taryn. And that's stereotyping, isn't it? Sort of what you were expecting when we arrived."

"We both were, Coop," she protested lightly. "And you can't tell me it didn't happen."

The car pulled up and Brent hopped out, loaded their bags and settled her inside with a jaunty tip of his hat. "Y'all have a great drive home. It was a pleasure serving you."

"Thanks again, Brent."

Revving the engine, he accelerated down and out of the driveway, relieved to be away from the Gleasons, though appreciative of their efforts. He just wondered how he'd done. Slanting a glance at Taryn, he amended the thought. How they'd done. High marks and comments aside, Monica's interest in him was sexual, not business, and he was well aware of a woman's proclivity toward spite and jealousy when it came to a man. Especially one she couldn't have.

He gripped the steering wheel tightly.

"Coop, you okay?" Taryn's mellow, husky voice poured over him like warm honey.

Just like that, the tension eased from him. Impulsively, he reached across the seats and picked up her hand, laying her palm flat over his thigh, stroking her silky skin with his fingers. "Yeah. How about you? You make out all right?"

Her nails dug into the thin fabric of his khaki's and he swore she purred but when he looked at her, only a small smile hovered at her lips. "Yes, I guess I did. I admit starting out I was ready for a fight, but not too many of the guests did that."

Her fingers relaxed and Coop nearly groaned as they splayed wider over his leg, dangerously close to his crotch. Any closer and she'd find out how hard he was. What the hell were they talking about?

"Coop?"

"Yeah?" He concentrated on the winding road dotted by evergreen trees and rustic, wooden fencing.

She sighed. "Just looking for a little conversation."

"Honey, if you want conversation, you'll have to move your hand."

She did and he grabbed it again, putting it back where it was. "On second thought, I'm sure I can talk this way. I'm great at multi-tasking, remember?"

Taryn's mind filled immediately with proof from last night. Coop's fingers and tongue driving her wild, while she pleasured him at the same time. Multi-tasking. "Mmm, yes, I definitely remember that." Though she didn't really want to, Taryn decided she ought to change the direction of their discussion. Coop was as hard now as he'd been several times last night. She looked around, double-checking to make sure there really wasn't a spot to pull over.

Nope. Damn the luck. Her wet factor

increased tenfold just thinking about last night.

"So," she cleared her throat and tried again, "what's your overall impression of the party?"

He chuckled. "It was good. Very, very good. A few blips, but nothing earth-shattering. How about you?"

"Hmm, aside from wanting to throttle Monica on a semi-regular basis, and that murder of crows who were always at her side, I'd say it went rather well."

"Murder of crows?"

She smiled at his dubious tone. "Yeah, you know, old hens? My mom always used to call the town busybodies that. A murder of crows."

"Ah, I see." He was quiet a moment, the rough pad of his fingertip on her hand sending goosebumps up her arm and straight to her nipples. "Taryn, I have to ask. It's been driving me nuts all weekend."

Uh-oh, that didn't sound good. "What?" she asked warily.

"How'd you do that? Is it from being in the theatre?"

"Huh? Coop, a little more explanation would help."

"Blend in so damn effortlessly," he said, head shaking. "Hell, I almost thought you were a chameleon."

Her stomach tightened again, that roiling, sick feeling rising to the back of her throat. For half a second, she feared she'd ralph on his leather seats. But she forced it back down. How much to tell him? Take the out he unknowingly gave her?

No, she couldn't do that. It wasn't in her nature to run. Not anymore.

"I became what they wanted, Coop. After a while, it becomes second nature." She tried to remain expressionless, but the car slowed and his hand flattened over hers.

"You make it sound like the most repulsive thing on the planet."

Damn, she didn't want to do this now. "It's not my favorite thing to do, no." Struggling for an answer that wasn't one, Taryn licked her lips and narrowed her eyes. "It was a necessity. What it took to get the job done."

He gave her a searching glance staring so long she grew nervous and waved toward the steering wheel.

"Drive, Coop,"

"I am. I'm also wondering why you dislike it so." A frown creased his brow. "I would think that mingling with the kind of guests at the Gleasons' would be a regular thing for you."

"Huh?"

"For the opera. Don't you do the whole fundraising thing?"

She chuckled. "Nope. I'm just the costumer, not the designer. Only the upper echelon gets invited to those soirees, which suits me fine." Taryn squeezed his thigh, enjoying both the freedom to do so and the rugged strength beneath her palm. "I'd rather party with the grunts I work with, anyway. Talk about fun."

"Yeah?"

"Yep, no expectations to live up to. No need to worry about saying or doing the wrong thing and being banned for life."

His thigh muscle tensed beneath her hand. He shifted slightly, the car accelerating down the open road. "Is that how you felt this weekend?"

Taryn hesitated, biting back her automatic "Of course."

"Taryn?"

"Not a whole lot, no. It really wasn't as bad as I thought it would be."

"Thank you," he said simply.

Scooting sideways in her seat, she pierced him with a questioning look. "For what?"

"For being honest." He downshifted, exiting the freeway and stopping at a red light. He looked at her, his hand slipping from the gear stick to settle on hers.

"Well, hell, Coop, it's not like they shackled me to the grass and tossed lawn darts my way. I'm a big girl, I have no problem admitting when I was wrong. There were moments of discomfort, yes, and I could have done without Monica, but overall it was okay." She shook her head. "Not that I'll repeat the experience."

The light changed and he took off. "So if I asked you to another event …"

Taryn slipped her hand away and looked out the window, glad they were almost to her house. Much as she'd enjoyed her time with him, this conversation was getting too close to her memories. The whole weekend had been one giant flashback. Coupled with fantastic sex, yes, but still… "I guess it depends on what it is. How about dinner?" she said, hoping to distract him.

"Or the movies. A play? A puppet show?"

Coop laughed. "Are you asking me out for a date?"

Taryn's breath caught. For all her semi-newfound strength, determination, and nights of fantasies starring Coop, asking him out sounded so...wrong. But he didn't seem opposed to the idea. Licking her lips, she nodded. "Sure."

"Great." Pulling into her driveway, he killed the engine, popped the latch on the trunk and turned to her, searching her face.

She raised a brow and winked. "Yes?"

He leaned close and cupped her jaw. His fingers stroked her skin and she nearly melted. "Nothing," he whispered against her mouth.

Taryn's lids fluttered closed and she concentrated on the shape of his lips, the way they melded and formed to hers. His light, soft touch soon was not enough and a whimper escaped her.

He pulled back. "What, baby?"

Reaching up, she fisted his shirt. "More."

The grin that formed was cocky, but she didn't care. Coop's mouth found hers again, the slight gruffness of his five o'clock shadow scraping erotically along her skin as he pressed harder, deepening the kiss. She moaned and opened her mouth, inviting him inside.

His tongue slipped along the bottom edge of her lip, teasing and taunting her. She shifted and tugged again on his shirt, darting her tongue out to find his.

Coop's groan of approval zipped into her mouth and she squeezed her eyes shut, savoring.

He kissed her soft, hard, long and slow, fast and sweet for what seemed hours. By the time he broke off, they were both gasping for air.

"We should go inside," she suggested, disentangling her hands from his thick hair.

"Yeah," he rasped as he dropped another soft kiss on her lips.

Heart racing, clit throbbing, Taryn shoved the door open and slid from the car, digging in her purse for the house key. The trunk thudded shut behind her and Coop dropped her suitcases in the entry as he followed her inside.

He kicked the door shut and wrapped his arms around her, snuggling her close to his body, hands roving her back and ass with a sure, deft touch that drove her need to fierce heights.

Her heart raced and skipped with each caress. She'd never felt this intensity before, this urgency. Only with him. She hesitated, pulling away from him slightly, swallowing hard.

Affair of convenience, she reminded herself. Fun, light, erotic. Fantasy come to life. Her heart was not to be involved.

She lifted her eyes, meeting his green gaze head-on, seeing the passion flaring deep in him. That hot, heated stare shot straight to her clit, forcing rational thought easily away. Licking her lips, she grabbed his hand and led him down the hallway to her bedroom.

"Come on, Tiger, let's get naked and wild."

Coop pressed a last lingering kiss on Taryn's mouth and slid from the bed, wearing only a sated grin.

"Mmm, you have to go already?" she protested in a mumble, smiling sleepily up at him.

Her mass of blond hair was a wild tangle caused both by his hands and the thrashing of her head as he'd moved inside her.

Damn, he was getting hard just thinking about it. Coop had half a mind to go back down to the bed and slide into her again. Damn. She was better than any little blue pill.

"I don't want to, baby, but I have to." With one last, crotch-stirring look at her sprawled so wantonly, he turned away, searching for his clothes. Lifting the comforter they'd managed to shove onto the floor, he snagged his boxer briefs and pants.

Stepping into them, he snuck another glance her direction, finding her lying with one arm across her hip, the other propping her head up. She watched him with hooded, come-hither eyes, full lips parted and moist. "Can I change your mind?"

Coop lifted his shirt from behind a dark brown chair and shrugged into it. "Hell, yeah."

She waggled her brows, rolled over on her back and tipped her head over the edge of the bed, hands sweeping over her chest, down the curve of her waist, settling on her hips. "Do you want me to?"

Torn between his need to get home and make sure his proposal for the Gleasons was complete and the picture of his tousled temptress laid out before him, Coop hesitated. Yes, he wanted her to, but he also needed to take care of business.

She sighed and sat up, pulling the sheet up and around her as she stood. Walking forward, she looped her arms about his neck, pressing a soft kiss to his jaw. "How about a rain check, Coop?"

Relieved regret raced through him. "I'm sorry, Taryn, I'd love to stay, but this deal with the Gleasons —"

"Shhh." She pressed her fingers to hips lips, smiling up at him, her silver eyes mischievous. "I understand. But I will collect on that rain check."

Coop smoothed his hands along her naked waist and back, grateful she wasn't putting up a fuss. "Name the day and time, baby, and I'll be there."

"Mmm, soon." She touched her lips to his, staring him in the eyes, her lashes dropping just a hint as her tongue swiped out. Her nostrils flared and the tips of her nails dipped into the skin at the back of his neck.

Coop opened his mouth, watching her intently, letting her take the lead, knowing it was idiotic to start this again. He had to get home. But she was hard to resist.

Her eyelids fluttered closed as she slid her tongue further inside his mouth and sealed their lips together. Fingers tightening on her waist, he inhaled sharply. She smelled of woman and sex, their scents mingling together to form a powerful aphrodisiac.

"To hell with the proposal," he whispered roughly against her lips, walking her back toward the bed.

Her eyes popped open and she pushed away. "No." Taryn's hands fell from his neck, flattening on his chest. "I'm sorry, I didn't mean for that to happen." A frown formed over her brows. "You're a little addictive, Mr. Malone."

She stepped back and wrapped the sheet tighter around her. Coop stifled a groan. If she was looking to ward him off, that was not the way to do it. The creamy linens molded to her body, outlining her beautiful breasts and hips with erotic precision.

"Coop?"

He grunted and looked down for his socks and shoes. One sock he wrestled from the cat, the other he found stuffed in his pocket. Looking up he caught the worried look on her face. "Hey." He cupped her shoulders, remaining out of body touching range. "It'll be okay. Really." He winked. "There's a 69-step program for addicts, you know."

Her husky chuckle washed over him, warming him and making his heart catch. His heart? Whoa, time to take to recoup. Literally. He squeezed her shoulders and stepped back, determined to keep it light. No way, no how was his heart involved after only a week. "I'm serious."

"Oh yeah, I bet. Where do I sign up?" She winked and turned to the tall dresser, pulling a long pink satiny nightshirt out.

Coop watched, captivated by the long, sleek

lines of her bare back as she slipped the gown over her head. The sheet dropped just before the pink material covered her butt, affording him a mouth-watering view of her firm cheeks.

"You are a dangerous woman, you know that?"

Taryn's wide-eyed, patently false innocent look made him grin. "I am?"

He nodded. "You ought to come with a warning label." Splaying his hands in front of him he said, "Warning—viewing this woman will cause perpetual hard-dick syndrome."

Though she laughed, he saw the blush that climbed into her cheeks. "Well, I'm glad you think so."

Mournfully, he looked down at his crotch. "Yeah. I think so. A lot. A painful lot."

She patted his jaw, scooting past him and picking up the cat. "You'll live."

"Are you sure about that?"

"Yep."

He nodded. "'kay. What are your plans for tomorrow?"

She sat on the edge of the bed, cuddling the cat to her chest, stroking its fur with long, graceful fingers.

Coop shifted, his slacks threatening to chafe even through his boxer briefs.

"We're starting a new production in a month and we've got a lot of design and construction work to do."

"I thought you didn't design?"

"I don't for the opera, but I wield a mean hammer." Taryn laughed. "I'm a regular girl

Bob Vila."

"Cool." Remembering the days of his drama past and the fun they'd had building sets, Coop felt a twinge of envious nostalgia. "If I didn't have to meet with the Gleasons, I'd drop by and lend a hand."

Her brows shot up and her eyes widened. "Don't be silly, we get all grungy and dirty and sweaty."

Coop set his jaw at the implied criticism. "I can get sweaty with the best of them, Taryn."

She purred, one hand sweeping over the bed. "Yes, I know."

He shook his head, the brief dart of irritation gone with her wicked smile. "Temptress."

Taryn bit her bottom lip, looking up at him through lowered lashes. "Sorry." The sultry way she said it told him she was anything but.

"I'm not." Leaning down, he kissed her hard and fast before stepping away. "But I do need to go. We'll continue this discussion later."

Taryn let Velvet jump to the floor, stood and followed Coop out of the bedroom, watching his butt move in his slacks.

Yum. She smothered a giggle with her hand, amazed at the exhilaration flying through her. Giddiness, happiness, repletion. That and more and she knew it was due to Coop's love-making. Going to bed with him was one of the best decisions she'd made.

Worth repeating my past?

Taryn stumbled slightly, catching herself on the wall of the hallway, nudging an old college picture. Straightening it, she found herself face-to-print with not only her old, submissive self, but her ex, as well.

The group of twelve in the picture were all his friends, all members of the elite club of future, prominent businessmen. They'd had big plans, and William's were the biggest of all. Tracing her finger over the severe black suit and hideously sensible shoes she wore, Taryn shook her head and pulled the picture down.

"Taryn?"

Coop's low, questioning voice brought her out of the fog of her past and she smiled up at him, holding the photo aloft. "Old memories."

He frowned, one hand on the doorknob. "Hell of a memory if it makes you scowl like that."

She nodded. "Yeah, it is."

"Why keep it?"

The words were so simple, so straight-forward she could have smacked herself for not asking them in the first place. With a wide grin that threatened to become a chuckle, she shook her head.

"Good question." Flipping it over, she pulled the cardboard backing off, peeled the print from the glass and gleefully tossed the black and white in the trash. Just like that, she thought. So easy. The way it should be.

Coop stepped toward her, peering into the rattan trash can. "What was it a picture of?"

"Just some idiots I knew in college. Not worth remembering, to tell you the truth."

Worth. The word bounced in her head and from left field the question hit her—was sleeping with Coop worth the potential for hurt his type offered?

"Hmm, don't know, Taryn." His hand cupped her jaw, imbuing her with a sweet sense of comfort. "You're still not smiling. What's bugging you?"

His eyes sparkled with sincere concern, the warmth of his hand strong and gentle on her skin.

He wasn't her ex. And more than likely, Cooper Malone was worth the risk.

Though she admitted that much, Taryn refused to look any further tonight. Too much had happened over the weekend for rational thought. She would take it as it came.

"Nothing, Coop, I'm just tired." She nipped at his finger, lowering her lid in a campy wink. "You wore me out, big boy."

He didn't look entirely convinced, his green eyes searching hers for a long, quiet moment. "I'm here if you need to talk."

"Thanks."

He sighed. "But you won't take me up on it?"

Spending the rest of the night spilling her guts about her disastrous ex-marriage appealed about as much as having a one-on-one conversation with Monica Gleason. "Not tonight."

"All right, I won't push. Just know that I've got broad, waterproof shoulders and a short memory."

Her heart fluttered wildly and she found it oddly hard to breathe. Damn, where had he been six years ago?

"Thanks, Coop." She raised up on tiptoe and pressed a soft, long kiss to his lips. "Now go home and read. I know you'll be up until midnight anyway, but you'll need some rest for the meeting."

He blinked as he nodded. "Hmm, I think you're starting to know me, Taryn."

Yeah, and the more she learned the more she liked. A damn scary thought. *Fun and light.*

With more frivolity than she felt, Taryn winked and opened the front door. "Sweet dreams, Coop."

"You, too, baby." A final, lingering kiss and he strode out the door, climbed into his car and backed out of the drive.

"You have no idea." She watched his taillights until they disappeared around the corner before going back inside and locking the house up.

Too restless to sleep, Taryn poured herself a glass of port and watched the fireflies flickering outside of her French doors. Heavy, seductive music swelled from the stereo as she sat and pondered.

Coop was not William, that much was clear. Where her ex would have ridiculed her adornments, Coop reveled in them. One hand toyed with her belly button piercing. Oh yes, he'd definitely liked that.

Coop was sexy, considerate and had a sense of humor. She took a large swallow of wine then licked her lips.

"Great Taryn, he's the perfect man. So,

what's wrong with you?"

Whispers of her past snuck in again. The old insecurity, the self-consciousness, the memory of being judged by her cup size instead of her intelligence. She'd had another taste of that world this weekend and hadn't liked it a bit. There was a reason she'd left that behind and she held no desire to return.

Only Coop made it worthwhile. Made it bearable. Just thinking about the nights of passion she'd experienced at his hands was enough to dampen her panties and cause her to shift restlessly on the couch.

"Looks like B.O.B. is going to get lucky." A spate of giggles, brought on by the stout wine, erupted from her. Standing, she trailed into the bedroom, rummaged in her bedside drawer and pulled out her favorite purple toy. "Hello B.O.B.," she cooed and sat down.

Taryn stripped her gown off, carelessly tossing it to the floor and laid back on her pillows, the vibrator clutched in one hand, her other arm draped over her eyes, shutting out everything but the delicious memory of Coop's hands on her body. In her body.

"Coop," she said on a sigh. Her fingers loosened their grip around the purple vibrator and it rolled to the floor, but she didn't feel like moving to retrieve it.

No, she wanted to relive again and again the many orgasms Coop's talented tongue had given her. Far better than a B.O.B. any day.

Sliding her hand between her legs, she let herself fall into a mix of dream fantasy and erotic reality.

Chapter Seven

"Spread your legs wider, baby," Coop muttered hoarsely as he bent her over the bed, his muscular body pressing against hers.

She complied, scooting her stiletto-clad feet as far apart as she could comfortably stand, groaning at the slight pull of her inner thighs.

His hand cupped her, fingers quickly finding her wetness, using it to ease themselves inside. Taryn's head lifted, eyes tightly shut as he moved his hand back and forth, slowly then with greater speed as she started to tremble.

"Coop," she gasped, so close to orgasm.

"Now, baby," he said in her ear and, riding his fingers and the incredible, shuddering explosion, she came hard.

Sawdust flew, hammers pounded and a general roar occupied the opera house as Taryn walked inside, body still ultra-sensitive from her overnight dream session with Coop.

"What's with the Cheshire grin, Taryn?" her friend Britt Ackerson asked. "And where'd you disappear to this weekend? I tried calling, but you didn't answer."

The statuesque red-head twirled a screwdriver like a small baton, brows raised.

Taryn winked.

Britt's eyes widened and she squealed, dropping the screwdriver and hauling Taryn into a bear hug. "You got laid!"

"Jeez, Britt, why don't you just get on the sound system so everyone can hear you?" Taryn poked her good-naturedly in the ribs, not in the least offended. "But yeah, I had a great weekend."

"Who? Do I know him? Where'd you meet him? Spill, chick!"

"Ladies, work and talk, work and talk," the stage director shouted, glaring in their direction. "C'mon, work with me here. Multi-tasking, multi-task!"

Taryn giggled. "We're going Art, keep your shorts on." She picked up the screwdriver and handed it to her friend, looking around for something to do. Spying a newly built fence in need of paint, she started forward only to be stopped by Britt's strong grip.

"Hold the boat, honey, you're not getting away that easily."

"Help me paint, then."

"Ugh." Britt looked down at her overalls. "But I'm in white." She pouted.

"That never works, Britt. You want to know, you gotta paint."

"Damn pain-in-the-ass." She sighed gustily. "Fine."

Grabbing the unfinished fence portion, a

bucket of paint and two brushes, the women hauled everything to a huge tarp spread on the floor and sat down.

"His name is Cooper Malone," Taryn said, prying open the lid with the screwdriver. "No, you don't know him, I met him here but I know him from Joe's."

"Joe's? Wait a sec... Coffee Guy?" Britt's eyes were as round as the can lid. "You finally scored with Coffee Guy? All right, Taryn. But how'd you meet him here?"

The run-down took the entire first coat of paint on her side of the fence. Though she normally shared everything with Britt, Taryn found herself editing the most salacious and private moments of her time with Coop. She frowned, wondering why. Hell, Britt was the one who gifted her with B.O.B., the purple warrior. They had no secrets from each other.

So, why now?

"Taryn." Britt's voice was caked with concern and hesitancy, something usually foreign to her friend. "Are you sure about this? He sounds a bit too much like William for my tastes."

Mercy smiled on her in the form of the delivery guy. "C'mon, pizza's here." Scrambling to her feet, she looked down at Britt who still frowned.

"Be careful, honey, that's all I'm asking."

Taryn nodded and headed for the boxes of pepperoni pizza. Yeah, careful was what she needed to be, but what if it was too late for that? The whirlwind of her relationship with Coop was in drastic contrast to the slow, methodical courtship of her marriage. Whether that was a good thing or not remained to be seen.

Worming her way into the feeding frenzy, she managed to snag a couple of pieces before they disappeared. Good-natured jostling and grumbling filtered around the table and she slowly relaxed. She loved being here, loved the atmosphere and these people who were more than co-workers. They were a family.

Sinking cross-legged onto the floor, she bit into her pizza, surveying the gaggle of friends. Dressed to the grungiest degree possible, they were well aware of the futility of wearing decent clothing to construction days.

Strung along the stage in ragged knots of three and four, Taryn eyed her friends, comparing this relaxing, laughter-filled gathering with the one she'd attended with Coop. Light year's difference.

There she became what they wanted. Here she was who *she* wanted to be.

Britt dropped next to her, a plateful of salad and one teeny slice of pepperoni-less pizza in hand. "So when you gonna see him again?"

"Don't know," Taryn mumbled around a bite. She supposed since she was the one who issued the rain-check it was up to her to make good on it.

"Why not?"

She shrugged. "He's busy working on a huge proposal."

Britt's nose wrinkled. "How William-esque."

Uncertainty slid down Taryn's shoulders like

cold water, leaving behind an uncomfortable feeling. "He's not," she insisted. "But this—"

"Is important," Britt finished with her. "Gee, where have you heard those words before?"

"Knock it off, Britt."

"Yo, Taryn, visitor." The resounding boom of Art's voice echoed over the stage and everyone's eyes whipped to the back.

"Huh?" She exchanged glances with Britt and slowly rose, cupping her hands over her eyes, trying to make out the figure standing at the end of the center aisle. Her heart sped up and her mouth dried as she recognized the broad shoulders. "Coop."

Coop stared back at the twenty-something pairs of curious eyes and resisted the urge to shift and tug at his tie. He got the feeling he was being weighed, maybe not judged, but definitely weighed. Was this how Taryn felt over the weekend? The thought made him sick to his stomach.

"Coop," she called, waving from stage left.

Starting down the plush, carpeted aisle, he met her in front of the orchestra pit. "Hi," he said, debating the wisdom of kissing her. He really, really wanted to, despite the fact he could still taste her sweetness from last night. It wasn't enough, he needed another fix.

"Hi," she replied, brushing a strand of hair from her face. "What are you doing here? I thought you were busy with the Gleasons."

He grimaced, feeling the knot of tension reforming between his shoulder blades. "They rescheduled. Again."

"Damn, I'm sorry."

"I'll get over it. Anyway, I thought I'd come over and see if you guys could use a hand."

She gaped, mouth dropping as she looked him over carefully. "Uh, well, you're not exactly dressed for it, Coop. You'll ruin your suit."

"It'll clean."

"I don't know, Coop."

The knot grew. Did she not want him here? He raised his eyes, finding the group assembled directly behind her, shamelessly, blatantly listening to the conversation.

"Taryn, you dork, never turn away free help," someone yelled.

"Yeah," a tall redhead concurred, spearing him with a hooded look. "Especially ones that look like that."

Taryn rolled her eyes, but a smile lifted her lips. "You did hear that word free, didn't you? I mean, we can offer pizza and soda, but that's it. And the actual presence of any remaining pizza is iffy."

He relaxed. "S'okay, I'll survive."

"Well..." she drawled.

"Taryn!" the group yelled in unison.

She laughed. "All right, all right. Darn busybodies." Motioning him forward, she whispered low in his ear. "I'm warning you now, you're going to be bombarded with lots of questions, comments and general goofiness. Take it all with a grain of salt. They're going to try and feel you out."

To hell with restraint. Coop brushed a kiss

along her cheek, to the tip of her nose and full against her lips, lingering on the salty softness, though a hint of her sweetness was still present. "Mmm, pepperoni." He pulled back. "Relax, Taryn, I can handle myself just fine."

"Hope so." She winked and grabbed his hand, pulling him on stage. "Okay, you miscreants listen up. This is Cooper Malone, a friend of mine."

Oohs and aahs, along with a few off-key comments issued from her friends and she waved them to silence.

"He's here to help, so be kind to him. Free labor is free labor."

"I bet he's great with his hands," a small dark-eyed girl offered with a sultry laugh.

"Can it, Rita, he's also off limits."

The girl pouted. "Spoilsport."

Taryn turned back to Coop and he caught her blush. "You said the same thing about my hands last night, baby," he whispered in her ear, enjoying the deepening of her rosy flush.

"Shush. Come on, let's go back to the dressing room. I'm sure we can find you something else to wear."

In short order, she had him decked out in a grungy, and a size too small t-shirt and carpenter pants that threatened to fall off until she tied a rope belt around him. Watching her small, deft hands work the rope, he thought of several other uses for it.

He wondered if he could swipe the belt.

"Coop." She halted him before they returned to the stage. "Are you sure about this? You don't have to. I mean, it's nice and all, but…"

"I want to be here, Taryn."

"Good." Her grin reflected vibrantly in her silver eyes. "Come on, free labor, let's put you to use."

"Promise?" he whispered, following her up the stairs, watching the way her butt swayed in the tight jeans.

She tossed him a grin and motioned him forward. "I'll introduce you to Art, the stage manager. He'll set you up wherever he needs you."

Coop started. He thought he'd be with her. "Uh, okay."

Art Lasko was a balding, rotund man clutching an unlit and mostly chewed stump of a cigar in his mouth. Despite the scowl piecing his brows together, he shook Coop's hand with enthusiasm. "Always use another hand. Let's see, where to put you?"

"Gotta run, Coop. Don't worry, I'll be around, keeping an eye on you." Taryn slid her hand around his waist, tugging on a belt loop before she walked away, straight for the tall redhead with the unreadable eyes.

He felt deserted and again wondered if this wasn't how she felt over the weekend. If so, he had some serious making up to do. He hadn't realized…

"So, what are you good with?"

Coop turned back to Art. "Uh, organization, mostly."

"Huh…" Art chewed on the cigar some more, rolling it from corner to corner of his mouth, slitted eyes even more squinty as he looked over the stage. "Can't rightly tell what's going on where, but just find someone who looks like they need help and dive in. Got some scenery to be painted and some electrical that needs wiring. No, can't have you doing that. Stupid laws." Art ambled off, still muttering, leaving Coop in the middle of the stage, very aware of the eyes watching him.

Slowly he turned, taking in the various groups and the projects they were working on. He continued this for several minutes, forming a plan, garnering ideas for a smoother, less time-consuming operation.

When he was sure he could speed up their progress with a minimum of effort, he approached Lasko who stood near a mobile podium off stage, going through papers.

"Art?"

"Yeah?" He didn't look up.

"I was wondering..." he hesitated, uncertainty whipping through him. No, he knew what he was doing. "You're crew is a bit scattered."

"Jeez, tell me about it. Too many things to get done, no time to plan properly." Art's heavy sigh blew a few loose papers to the ground. With a curse and a groan, he stooped to retrieve them. "I need two months, they give me twenty-seven days. How am I supposed to do that? Always do, though. 'Course there was that little problem we had last time with the turret. Damn thing kept falling over. Had to use duct tape finally. Gotta love that duct tape."

Coop cleared his throat. "Yeah, it's good. But I think I have an idea of how to streamline, something that'll help it all get done smoother and faster."

Lasko's head popped up like a zit on a sixteen-year-old's nose. "Yeah?" He pulled his cigar out, eagerness on his face. "Feel like sharing?"

Coop relaxed, finally feeling as though he were not an interloper. "Yeah," he parroted with a grin.

Detailing his plan to Art took a few minutes, some quick sketches and earned him a hearty clap on the back from the stage director's meaty hand.

In less time than it took to brew a pot of coffee, Art had the entire stage re-configured according to his suggestions with crews assembled and working smoothly within the hour.

Catching Taryn's eye, he winked, pleased when she laughed and winked back, sending him a thumbs up. The redhead by her side finally cracked a smile as well, nodding slightly. Did that mean he passed muster?

"Hey, Coop, come on over here and help us with this router, would you?"

Striding toward the trio of men, he found himself pulled into their project with ease. They took turns holding the plywood and using the router to cut out the patterns drawn onto the wood in black marker. Squinting, he couldn't tell what it would be.

"What is it?"

Brian, the sandy-haired hulk wielding the power tool, looked down and grinned. "Hell if we know. We just do the cutting." He nodded to the left. "They do the assembling. Good plan you had, you know, getting all these stations going."

"Yeah, man, thanks."

Coop shrugged uncomfortably, shoving his hands in the pockets of his borrowed jeans. "Sure, no problem."

"So how long have you known Taryn?"

The question came from left field with no subtlety behind it whatsoever. The asker, a dark haired, slender kid of about twenty, stared at him frankly.

"A while." Not the whole truth, but enough. He'd seen her enough at Joe's to make it more true than not.

"Been dating her long?"

"No, not really."

"She's amazing, man. Great head on her shoulders. Funny, smart, gorgeous, outrageous."

The other men nodded and Coop's gut tightened slightly. He was starting to realize those qualities about her, but he hadn't had enough time yet to fully explore them. These guys knew her well.

"She's cool, Coop," the twenty-year old chimed in. "The things she's done…"

"Like?"

"Well, that Harley for one thing. Sex on wheels, that's our Taryn."

Coop's brow rose at the blatant lust in the youngster's voice.

"Don't mind Ritchie, he's got the hots for just about every female in the company," Brian assured him. "Taryn is very good at making them her friends, you know. All of 'em. And believe me, they've all tried."

Understanding dawned. "Including you?"

Brian gave a crack of laughter. "Yeah, me, too. I'm not immune to her charms, but she's never been romantically involved with anyone here."

"Thanks."

Brian grinned. "No problem, man. She's a pistol that one, but she deserves to be happy."

Happy? He looked around and spotted Taryn on top of a ladder, paint bucket in one hand, swiping at a tall piece of tree with the other. She smiled down at her statuesque friend, obviously saying something funny because the redhead laughed throatily.

Brian groaned. "I hate it when Britt does that."

"Britt?"

"The redhead with Taryn. That laugh always goes straight to my—"

"Can it, Brian," one of the guys said with a chuckle. "We know where it goes, you're practically moving the whole damn table."

Coop smiled with the rest of them and continued to watch Taryn. The remainder of the afternoon was spent in much the same fashion, him going from project to project as he was called for, fielding questions and watching her.

This was a side of her he'd not seen at the Gleasons. Here she was always smiling, always laughing, always happy. She didn't frown once, even when Britt accidentally splashed green paint over her aqua-colored sneakers.

She fit in here. This was who she truly was. Why did that sudden bolt of understanding cause the pit of his stomach to whirl and tighten?

She belonged here and it was obvious. Making even more obvious the fact that she really had been playing a role over the weekend. Brilliantly played, but not her true self by any stretch. If she'd displayed this much warmth and wit to the people at the Gleason's, they would never have been allowed to leave.

"Hey Coop!"

He sighed, tearing his gaze away from Taryn and searching for the voice now calling him. Rita, the small Latina girl, waved at him. Walking over, he raised a brow. "Yes?"

"What are you doing this weekend?"

"I'm sure Taryn and I have plans," he said neutrally.

She beamed. "Oh, you'll be with Taryn. Great, then we'll see you at the Faire?"

"Faire?" he repeated, feeling more like a parrot as the afternoon wore on.

"The Renaissance Faire. While we're not in production, a bunch of us go out there and do some costume stuff. We do a bit of acting and entertaining. It's loads of fun."

The excitement on her face gave testimony to her enthusiasm and Coop found himself grinning back. "What, like you dress up in outfits and eat turkey legs?"

Rita laughed. "There's more to it than that, but I'm sure Taryn'll fill you in before you get there."

"Fill him in on what?" Taryn's sultry voice slid up his spine and he looked down at her, a welcoming smile on his face.

"Hey," he said softly, wrapping his arm around her waist.

She leaned into him. "Hey, yourself. What am I filling you in on?"

"The Ren Faire," Rita said, checking her watch. "Hey, look at that, quitting time. Excellent. See you tomorrow, Taryn. Coop, hope to see you at the Faire."

"Yeah, thanks. You, too."

She darted off and he realized the stage was mostly deserted, only he, Taryn, Brian and Britt remained.

"You want to go to the Faire?" Taryn asked skeptically.

"Why not?"

"Well, it doesn't really seem like your sort of thing."

He was getting tired of being typecast as the dull one. "I want to go. What time do I pick you up?"

"Uh, well, Coop…"

He set his jaw. "Don't you dare ask me if I'm sure, Taryn. I want to go and experience this with you. You lead, I'll follow. I'll do whatever you say. What time?"

Her eyes sparkled. "I lead, huh? What I say goes?"

"Yes," he said, wondering if he'd been a bit

foolhardy when her soft lips parted on a wide smile. "This time."

"Pick me up at seven on Saturday."

"Why so early?"

She winked, her hand dipping into the loose waistband of his jeans. "I'm dying to see you in a pair of tights."

"Tights?" he repeated on a strangled groan.

"Oh yeah." Her hand slipping from where it caressed his butt to the front of his boxer briefs. "Form-fitting and sexy as hell."

He closed his eyes, trying to concentrate on what she was saying and not what her deft hand was doing to his rapidly growing erection.

"Good thing these pants are so loose, Coop."

"Witch," he muttered, pulling her hand out. "What do you say we move this elsewhere?"

She licked her lips, eyelids half-lowered. "Okay, Tiger, but this time, you strip for me."

He grinned. "Deal."

Chapter Eight

"Welcome my lady, good sir."

Coop eyed the small, bearded man standing at the side gate. Dressed in dark purple leggings, a blousy cream-colored tunic tied with a leather strip around his small waist and a hat in the same color as his leggings fitted with a feather, he looked as though he could have stepped from the fifteenth century.

Except for the round, gold wire rim glasses on his face.

"Hi Dell, how's tricks?"

"Fair to middlin', gentle lady." The guy leaned forward. "Watch out for Murray and Jeff. They're in a catfight."

"Oy." Taryn nodded. "Thanks for the tip. Come on, Coop, let's suit up."

"Y'all have fun," the odd little man called as they walked away.

Coop tried to take in the quickly passing scenery, but Taryn's pace didn't let up enough to get a good visual. "Who are Murray and Jeff? And where we headed?"

"They're comic jugglers."

Coop laughed. "They juggle comics?"

She giggled, sending him an eye-rolling look. "No, silly, they juggle and are funny at the same time. And we're going to the dress building. It's where all the entertainers get ready for the day." She winked at him. "I can't wait to see you in your tights, Coop."

The cat-fighting comics were promptly forgotten. "Uh, Taryn, about those tights…"

"No weasling, Malone. You promised."

She stopped in front of a low-slung wooden building painted in bright yellow with a red-and-green Celtic border along its walls. A canvas awning jutted out from it. "You will be wearing them if I have to pour you into them myself."

He laughed. "If that's a threat, it's not working." Stepping next to her, he wrapped his arm around her waist. "You get pour me into anything you want."

She shoved him with her shoulder. "Come on, Coop, let's go change." Grabbing hold of his hand, she dragged him through the canvas archway and into the dimly-lit room.

He didn't know what he expected, but chaos certainly wasn't it. Dressing rooms, privacy, hell even a football-style locker room, perhaps. But not mobile racks filled to bending with various gowns and tunics or boxes overflowing with props and accessories. Taryn zeroed in on a free-standing rack, tugging the multi-colored clothing this way and that.

Squatting, he riffled through one of the

boxes, shaking his head at the plethora of strange hats. He lifted one out, a tall, pointed green thing with blue, black and yellow ribbons. It jingled when he turned it. "Good grief," he said, spying the small bells tied at the end of the ribbons. "Did people really wear this crap?"

"A-ha! Oh, yeah, this is perfect." She turned, arms clutched over a wad of material. "And yes, plenty wore that. I think."

Coop dropped the hat and stood, eyeing the clothes. "I'm afraid to ask, but what did you find?"

She batted her eyes at him. "Why Cooper... What's your middle name, anyway?"

"Huh?"

"Middle name. The one after the first, before the last?"

Coop raised a brow and stalked forward, crowding her against the rack, cupping her chin in his hand. "Sassy, aren't we?"

She thrust her hips forward. "Why, you plan on doing something about it?"

He smacked her playfully on the behind. "Maybe. It's Jarod."

Taryn's grin was wide and genuine. "Cooper Jarod Malone, 'tis a right fine sounding name, my lord."

He winced. "No offense, but that's got to be the worst attempt at a British accent I've ever heard."

Taryn stuck her tongue out. "Bite me. Now then, Cooper Jarod Malone, don't you trust me?"

"Only a fool trusts a beautiful woman."

Her ice-blue eyes widened.

He lifted his finger to her lips, silencing her. "And I've often been called a fool."

"Oh, you are good." She pushed at his chest. "Go on, change, Coop, while I find something to wear myself."

"Where do I change?"

"Right here, unfortunately. Do it quick, if you're shy. No one is likely to come in this early."

"Likely to," he muttered as she flounced to the back of the room. Holding out the pieces she gave to him, he shook his head again. A ridiculously small pair of dark green pants, he flat-out refused to call them tights, paired with a huge shirt in the same creamy color as the guy at the gate. The throat was open damn near to his navel and the sleeves had floppy, frilly ends.

"Taryn," he roared. "I am not wearing this ... this..."

"It's called a shirt, Coop and yes, you are. You promised." Her voice floated out from the racks of clothing. "Come on." This time it was slightly muffled and he thought he heard her curse. "It'll be fun. Where's your spirit for adventure?"

Adventure? He had plenty of that. Didn't he? Hefting the clothes, he sighed. "What the hell, why not?"

Shucking his jeans and T-shirt, he pulled the pants on. His boxer briefs bunched in uncomfortable places and he found himself re-arranging body parts he'd rather not.

"Gonna have to take 'em off, Tiger. Besides,

there's a built-in codpiece."

He glared in the direction of her laughter. "Funny girl." But she was right. There was no way he was spending the entire day tramping around this place with a wedgie. Doffing the leggings, he stripped off his briefs and hastily pulled the green pants back on. Taryn's wolf-whistle was loud.

"Well, hell, Coop, that wasn't much of a show."

"Private performances are available for a small fee," he called out, adjusting the cup over his crotch. "Huh, not bad." He slid the shirt over his head, frowning at just how much it showed. Half his chest was exposed.

"Quit fussin' with it, my lord, ye look fine."

Coop turned, stared and had to adjust his suddenly uncomfortable codpiece. Taryn stood before him, one hand settled on her hip that cocked jauntily out, the other twirling a lock of her golden hair. But it was the outfit she'd donned that grabbed his attention and held him hotter than hell. He was so hard he threatened to burst through the leather cod piece now strangling his cock.

A white, peasant blouse dipped low on her bare shoulders while a green lace-up corset cinched her waist even smaller and lifted her luscious breasts high on her chest. The tops quivered enticingly with each breath she took. The full skirt she wore was in the same shade of green and had strategically placed ties that lifted the material, affording glimpses of long, tanned thighs. On her feet she wore black slipper-looking things with ribbons that wrapped up her calves, drawing his eye even more.

She looked exactly like what he imagined a saucy wench would. And then some.

"You like?"

"Hell yeah," he rasped, moving closer. Sliding his hands around her waist, he stroked the soft material covering her butt and looked down at the wide expanse of her nearly bare chest. "You look amazing."

She giggled. "What color are my eyes?"

"Brown," he stated quickly, catching her hand when she would have whacked him. Dropping a kiss on the tip of her nose, he rubbed his cheek against hers, inhaling her fragrance, enjoying the moment. "They are the most incredible shade of blue I've ever seen. Like sapphires melted into silver."

"Oooh, you wonderful, wonderful man." She sighed and cupped his face, kissing him long and hard. When she pulled away they were both gasping for breath. "C'mon, Coop, we need to get out of here or you'll never see the Faire."

"Suits me fine." He wanted nothing more than to lay her atop the glittering gowns on the floor and ravish her, just as a debauched lord of old would have done.

With another laugh, she tugged on his hand. "This way."

He followed her, enjoying the lush sway of her hips, exaggerated by the yards of material draping over her tight ass. "These costumes are great. Very well made."

She winked over her shoulder at him.

"Thanks."

He stopped, pulling her to a standstill as well. "You made these?"

"Uh-huh. C'mon, Coop, Murray and Jeff should be just about to start their first performance."

"Walk and talk, Taryn." Offering his arm, he fingered the cotton of her sleeve. "You do amazing work."

A blush tinted her fair cheeks and her ringlets swung as she tipped her head away. "Thank you."

"How many of the costumes did you make?"

She shrugged. "A few of them and I..." she trailed off, gazing away again.

"You what?"

"Never mind."

"Tell me." He gentled his voice at her raised brow. "Please?" Coop couldn't explain the need to know everything about her, nor did he give a damn about trying to figure that out. Right now, all he knew was that she made him feel alive. The proverbial breath of fresh air that seemed to lighten his life and his mood. Not to mention the incredible sex.

"Damn, you're a bulldog," she grumbled. Pushing her hair back, she twirled a locket around her finger, chin pointed up almost defensively. "I designed all the clothes for this year's Faire."

"You did?" Looking around at the various players behind wooden counters hawking their wares, rag tag "urchins" running through the crowds and the myriad other medievally-clad

Faire members, his respect grew. As did his confusion.

"Design? I thought you didn't do that."

"I don't at the opera. Don't have enough qualifications." Though her tone didn't really change, Coop sensed the subject was one that needled her. "But here they don't care about that as long as it's historically accurate."

"So this is what you're going to branch out into?"

She rolled her eyes and veered to the left, cutting across an already summer-burned patch of grass. "I'm happy at the opera, this is just something I do for fun."

"Fun that could make you a lot of money."

"Money is not the end all, be all, Coop. It's just a means."

"What about recognition? Ambition?"

She swung around, planting her fists on her hips, a deep frown etched on her brow. "I get plenty of recognition from the opera and my definition of ambition is probably way different than yours. I am content and that means more than money to me."

Coop heard the defensive frustration in her voice. Recognizing a frazzled nerve when he saw it, he decided to drop the subject. For now.

"Okay, wench, let's go find some entertainment!" He spun her around and smacked her butt, eliciting a sound halfway between a giggle and a growl.

With obvious relief, she crooked her finger at him. "This way, my lord, to the world's worst jugglers."

Wending their way through the growing throng of Faire visitors, they reached a large wooden stage fronted by rows of rickety looking benches. A large, straw covered canopy arched over the seats, providing some relief from the climbing Texas summer sun.

"Let's sit back here or else we'll end up in the show," she murmured out of the side of her mouth, motioning him to the back of the seats.

"Good thinking," he replied, sitting next to her.

"Yeah, especially when they start tossing the fire sticks."

His laugh was obscured by the blare of a loud, badly blown trumpet. Two men in technicolor outfits tumbled onto the stage. Apparently Jeff and Murray were also gymnasts. Though the men were funny, Coop couldn't keep his eyes away from Taryn, enjoying her reactions to their frivolity. Her laughter was genuine, face relaxed, smile wide. The utter happiness in her was infectious and he felt it seeping into him as well. He couldn't remember the last time he'd been this relaxed.

He also loved the way her lush breasts moved so enticingly with each laugh. Talk about perks. Why in the world corsets and low-cut peasant blouses fell out of favor, he didn't have a clue. They sure had his vote.

When Jeff, or was it Murray, picked up a passel of blackened torches, Taryn nudged him in the ribs. "That's our cue to leave. Last time they nearly caught the canopy on fire."

Coop stood and led the way back into the hot

sunshine. Looking down at her kissable lips, he nearly forgot what he meant to say. Tearing his gaze from her tempting mouth, he glanced around. "Where to next?"

"Let's just walk and see. Different events happen at different times."

"Works for me." Sliding his hand down her arm, he entwined their fingers, reeling at the rightness of it. At the easy familiarity they'd already developed. He cleared his throat. "What sort of events?"

Taryn's blue eyes peered at him quizzically for a moment before she tightened her fingers over his. "There's a joust, dancing, artisan demonstrations, music. Stage shows just about every hour or so. And wandering folk, too, for visitors and such. Crowd interaction is a huge part of the Faire's success. Dressed as we are, don't be surprised if someone wants to take our picture."

"Pictures?" He balked.

"Aye, my lord. 'tis what it's all about, ye know."

"No, I didn't know." And he wasn't sure how he felt about it. Dressing up and parading around for Taryn was one thing, but having his tights-clad image preserved for all time was another. He sure as hell didn't want them plastered all over the internet on some damn social media site. *It'd be just my luck those pictures would go viral.* What if his business associates got wind of it? How would they react? He couldn't imagine Monica or Troy Gleason in this atmosphere, that's for sure.

"C'mon, Coop, it's not that bad. I'll protect you." She pressed her body along his, sliding her arms up his neck, tugging lightly on his hair.

He automatically cupped her hips, fingers spread along her lush butt, trepidation fading, even if it didn't disappear altogether. "You will, huh?"

"Aye," she whispered, rising on tiptoe, lids fluttering closed.

Coop lowered his head, brushing her lips lightly, but before he could deepen the kiss, she was wrenched from his arms.

"What foul deed is this, sir?" a furious male voice asked.

Coop frowned harshly at the man standing in front of him, looking not even remotely ridiculous in his midnight-blue leggings and jerkin. His clothing, though similar in style to Coop's, spoke of a higher class. A sword hung in a sheath at his waist.

Taryn stood next to the man, a smile playing about her nearly-kissed lips. She tipped her head in the stranger's direction and mouthed "play along."

Play along, huh? He could do that. He needed to taste her again and he would not be denied.

"Who are you?" he demanded, glaring at the man in blue.

"I am Sir Reginald and this maid is under my protection. You have besmirched her honor and I demand satisfaction. Name yourself!"

A crowd gathered around them, murmuring with delight and excitement. Coop tugged at his collar, took in the fluttering, pleading eyelashes Taryn batted at him with impish delight and gave it a stab. "I am Sir Jarod and your implications slur her honor, you cretin."

Cretin? Hey that was pretty good. An ever-increasing sense of familiar spontaneity filled him. He stalked forward, reaching around Reginald to pull Taryn back to his side. "Satisfaction will be mine."

She giggled and he stifled a grin at the unintentional double entendre.

Reginald stiffened. "I'll not fight an unarmed man. Squire!" he yelled and a tow-headed lad of about nine raced forward, brandishing a sword.

Reginald nodded at Coop. "To my opponent, boy."

Coop took the sword, somewhat relieved to find it made of a lightweight material that didn't seem to be metal. He had no desire to be skewered.

Reginald leaned forward, motioning at Coop who did the same. "You fence?"

"Not really."

"Okay, keep your sword up and don't slash, just wave it gently. After a few strokes, I'll dip my blade and you'll knock mine from my hand for the win."

Coop found himself wanting to protest the rigged contest, but thought better of it. He really needed to kiss Taryn. "Got it."

"*En garde*," Sir Reginald shouted, flinging one hand in the air, sword pointed to the sky.

Coop mimicked his stance. His opponent nodded and Coop lunged forward, striking the other sword with a loud clatter. The crowd cheered in response and he continued the attack, beating the knight back a few paces before losing ground himself. When Reginald lowered his sword, Coop swiped at it, pleased when the blade flew to the ground, skittering across the grass.

Reginald knelt, head bowed. "You have won the day and nobly defended your lady's honor, good Sir Jarod."

His lady. He liked that. Coop lifted the other man's sword and returned it to him. "Perhaps next time you will reconsider such rash actions," he advised, thoroughly enjoying this step outside his normal world. "Now begone."

The knight bowed his head, thumping his heart with a closed fist. "Good day, sir, fair lady, good people."

The crowd cheered as he stood, turned neatly on his heel and strode away.

Taryn's hand slipped around Coop's waist, demanding his attention. When he looked down, she had an impish grin on her face that his tightened his gut for more than one reason. Desire, certainly, but he was beginning to realize that look meant trouble. Usually for him.

"My lord, how may I repay your bravery?"

The batting eyes and slow tongue slide across her bottom lip told him what she wanted him to say. With more than a hint of self-consciousness, Coop glanced at the crowd.

"Uh…"

"A kiss!" someone shouted. The cry was quickly taken up and soon a chant *of kiss the wench* reverberated around him.

"Come on, Coop," she whispered, licking her lips again. "Kiss me."

It was the tongue that did it. He wrapped his hands around her waist, tipped her chin up and slowly lowered his head, anticipating the sweet taste of her mouth with every slow inch he descended.

"God, Coop, you're driving me crazy," she muttered breathlessly.

"Good," he said just before fitting his mouth tenderly to hers. With a leisurely calm that belied his racing heart and rapidly engorging hardness, he kissed her. The softness of her lips tempted him, beckoned him to delve further and deeper. Enfolding Taryn's slender body in his arms, he nipped lightly at her mouth, slipping his tongue inside when she moaned in response.

Her eager response only served to shoot his desire higher, hotter. Hands sweeping over her back, he ground his hips into hers, fingers crushing the many layers of her dress that covered her buttocks.

Only a sharp wolf whistle brought him back to reality. To the realization that he, Cooper Malone, upstanding businessman, stood in a pair of damn tight leggings, kissing a seductive woman in front of a horde of strangers. And liked it. Wanted more of it. But not now.

"Later," he whispered against her ear.

She nodded, her cheek pressed to his chest. He knew she had to feel his blood pounding through him, feel the excitement she raised in him. There was no way Taryn could be unaware of the power she held over him. That thought alone was enough to rapidly cool his blood, but looking up he caught sight of an almost-familiar face which completely chilled it.

Brows knitted, he tried to place the face, but the man disappeared before he could name him.

The well-wishers closed in on them as he searched for the guy and he decided it was a trick of his imagination. He shook hands and posed for pictures until Taryn managed to ease them out of the throng's grasp.

"You did great, Coop," she exclaimed when they were alone again. Hugging his arm, she patted his butt. "And you look awesome in those tights. But what was with the Sir Jarod routine?"

Not wanting to address his attempt at anonymity, he waggled his brows. "I bet you look better in those leather chaps of yours. And nothing else."

Taryn's cheeks pinkened and her breathing changed, becoming faster. "You think so?"

"As often as I've imagined that over the past few days, baby, you'd better believe it."

"Hmm." She winked. "We'll have to see what we can do about that happening then."

He inhaled sharply, his vision of her chap-clad and bent over his couch instantly getting him hard again. "Damn."

"I'm gonna take that as a good damn."

"Oh yeah," he muttered, squeezing her shoulders lightly. "Since we can't feed that hunger, how about my stomach? All that fighting left me starving."

"Right this way, my lord. I know a right fine

place for victuals."

"Victuals, huh? I'll settle for decent food, but lead on."

She laughed and hauled him down the dirt path that connected all the different areas of the Faire. On the way they passed a giant of a man, as tall as a tree and nearly as broad in the chest as a redwood. He had greasy red hair, squinty black eyes and appeared to be missing half the teeth in his mouth.

"An ogre," Taryn murmured as they drew nearer. "His only purpose is to insult people."

"Good grief, who would tangle with him? The man's enormous. It's not natural."

Taryn laughed. "Want me to tell you why?"

Coop studied the ogre for a long minute before nodding. "I have a weakness for curiosity. I hate not knowing."

"Stilts and padding."

"Ah, makes sense."

"Yeah, well, let's skirt the crowd so he doesn't decide to make us his next victims."

"I've already battled this day, fair maiden." He stopped, letting a group of youngsters tear by him, keeping one wary eye on the ogre.

"Which means?"

"Well, here it may be fourteen-whatever, but in my book equality is alive and well. You get into a war of words with him."

"Nah," she shook her head. "I can never one-up him and it drives me nuts. Hey, look at that! Oh, come on, let's do it."

There she went again, tossing out that phrase that heated his blood with the mere thought of possibility. Somehow though, he knew she didn't mean what he wanted her to mean. "What?" he asked.

"A face-painting booth. We can get matching somethings."

"How about you get something and I'll admire it?"

She stood in front of the small kiosk, eagerly flipping through the design book. "Aw, please? Pretty please?" She batted her eyes at him.

"Not fair, wench."

She didn't let up and he growled at her before giving in, warning her not to pick a damn girly design. She chose dragons. A green one for him, silver for her.

The artist was mercifully quick and in no time they were en route to their dinner once more, matching fire breathing dragons now on their right cheeks. How did she do it?

No one else in the world could get him to indulge in such ridiculousness as she'd done today. But it felt good. Freeing and fun. More fun than he'd had in a decade at least. If then.

Her happiness was infectious and he was beginning to hope there wasn't a cure.

She moved him in ways no woman ever had. She was the first thing he thought of in the morning, the last at night.

"What do you fancy for eatin', my lord?"

Coop dragged himself away from that dangerous, scary line of thinking and perused the menu. "A turkey leg, I guess, and a beer. How about you?"

"The same, good sir. Oh hey, the Scottish

band is about to start, too. If we hurry we can just catch the final concert of the evening."

Coop stepped up to the counter and placed their orders, unable to believe the day had blown by so quickly. Time seemed unstable when he was with her. Quick as moonlight one minute, slow as the Texas sun the next.

Carrying their dripping, foil-wrapped feast and tall yards of ale, they found a comfortable spot on the grass and listened to the band tune their instruments.

Starving, Coop devoured his meal and was wishing for more when Taryn offered the remaining half of hers.

"Go on," she urged. "I never can finish them. Too much meat for me."

He smiled his thanks and polished off the succulent turkey in record time. He'd just returned from trashing the foil and napkins when the band began to play.

Immediately captivated by the haunting strains of the Celtic music, Coop couldn't resist pulling Taryn into his arms, settling her back to his chest and resting his chin on the top of her silken blond crown.

It felt right. She felt right in his arms. Like coming home after a long night. Damned if it didn't scare the hell out of him. He didn't want to examine his feelings, didn't want to dive any further into the idea that his affair might be developing into something much deeper and emotionally charged than he'd planned on. But he couldn't escape the truth. Refused to play the ostrich and hide from himself or his feelings.

In the brutal light of honesty, Coop realized he was falling in love with Taryn. Problem was, he didn't know what to do about it.

"That was beautiful," Taryn murmured.

He looked up to find the band packing up their instruments and talking with audience members as they crowded the stage.

"Yeah, it was great." He stood, pulling her to her feet, holding her still and drinking in the pleasure of her. Could this really be love? His heart spasmed and his throat constricted.

"You okay?" she whispered, stroking his jaw, her silver eyes anxiously searching his.

"Yeah," he murmured. "I'm fine." God, he hoped so. "What do you say we blow this pop stand and get back into our clothes? These tights are starting to constrict parts that ought not to be constricted, if you know what I mean?"

She laughed as he'd meant for her to do, and nodded. "Good idea."

Meandering hand in hand through the dispersing crowd, Coop again caught sight of the familiar face, this time able to put a name to the man. He groaned. Gary Bentley, a hard-nosed conservative with the amusement tolerance of a gnat. What was he doing here?

"Malone," Bentley nodded, blatantly looking him up and down. "Nice outfit."

"Mr. Bentley. How are you?"

The man was dressed in khaki's and a button-down shirt despite the heat of the day.

"Good. We were just leaving." Coop noticed a well-rounded redhead by his side, two smaller versions of her hiding behind her legs. He mustered a smile. "Hello Mrs. Bentley, kids."

She smiled. "Mr. Malone. Love the tights." Her grin grew.

His unease did as well. "Uh, thank you. I was just on my way to change. I was wearing them for a friend, just this once, you understand." He floundered to silence, knowing he was screwing it all up, but unable to prevent it. What the hell was wrong with him?

"We won't keep you, then. Good night." Bentley turned on his heel and stalked away.

"Who was that?" Taryn asked.

"A client," he sighed, wondering how much damage control he was going to have to do. Talk about appearing unprofessional. Bentley controlled large chunks of the local hotel market. A market that Coop kept under tight rein for him. Would that change? His attitude could barely be called chilly. Arctic was more like it.

Had he sunk himself by parading around in the tights?

"Let's change, Coop, and go home, okay?" Taryn's voice sounded as though it came from miles away instead of his side. He let her lead him back to the tent where he changed, unable to get Bentley's derisive look from his mind. The possibilities and what-ifs were driving him crazy.

The more he mulled over the situation, the quieter he became, and by the time they reached Taryn's door, he knew he'd not said more than a dozen words.

To her credit, she didn't complain. He

couldn't decide if it made matters worse that she seemed to understand the seriousness of what had occurred with Bentley. Or more to the point, what might occur.

He knew he was acting like an over-sensitive jackass, but Coop felt unable to stop it. His business was his life. Falling in love couldn't ruin that, no matter what.

Chapter Nine

"Are you coming in?" Taryn asked at her front door, anxiety gnawing at her. Coop's silence on the ride home fueled her doubts about their relationship, such as it was. What had begun as a fun, sexy fling was turning into something that had the potential to hurt her. Again.

Unlike her marriage, though, Taryn didn't want this to end. Not yet. Even if she wasn't certain the possible pain was worth the pleasure she found in his company and his arms. All she needed to do was keep her heart protected, her emotions firmly in check and she would be fine. She refused to think that it might be too late for such precautions.

"You still want me to?" he asked, surprise clear in his voice. The golden porch light spilled over him, highlighting the worry in his eyes, the downturn of his mouth and the stitched brows.

"Of course I want you to come inside, Coop. It's been a long day." With a deep breath, she trailed her finger along his open collar. "I thought we could... relax."

His face cleared up, though the worry in his eyes still lingered. Well, she would take care of that. Hooking her thumb in his belt, she tugged hard. "Come on, Tiger. I'll give you a full body massage and make you forget all about what's bothering you."

Coop's warm hand closed over hers, and his fingers caressed her jaw, eliciting sparks of tenderness mingled with sexual awareness. Her breath jerked and stilled just at this feathery touch.

"I'm sorry, Taryn."

"For what?"

"For the silent treatment on the way home. It's just seeing Bentley while I was dressed like that made it all crystallize in my head."

"Hey, he was there, too, Coop."

"Yeah, but he was not in tights and showing half his chest."

"Thank God for small favors."

Coop's face relaxed and his eyes crinkled, lighting with real amusement. "Yeah, there is that. I'm sure it's not that big of a deal."

Her doubt must have showed on her face because he dropped a kiss on her lips, tapped her nose and whispered, "Really."

Taryn smiled, hands working the buttons of his shirt. "Since we have that settled, why don't we go inside and get something else straight between us?"

The corny line had the desired effect and he laughed, firmly erasing all gloom in his mood. His big hands settled on her shoulders and he guided her backward into the foyer. Velvet rumbled a welcome home purr, wrapping in and out of their legs, but Taryn didn't stoop to pick her up, didn't want to lose the momentum building. After a few more head butts, Velvet meowed loud displeasure and huffed away, disappearing into the living room.

Coop's eyes, now smoldering, remained locked and steady on hers. From the desire sparking out of his green eyes, she knew something was on his mind. And judging from the bulge in his slacks, it was something sinfully fun.

"Tell me what you want," Taryn whispered, stroking his arms, his chest, up his neck. She loved to touch him.

A slow, sensual smile lifted his lips and flared deep in his eyes. "I want you."

"How?"

His hands dropped to her hips, clutching firmly, fingers massaging her through her jeans. "Bent over the couch, looking back at me with those beautiful eyes and incredible mouth." Intensity seared his face and his thumbs dug into her hipbones. "Wearing only your chaps."

"Oh God," she managed on a strangled breath as his vision hit her full force between her legs. The image of her so wantonly displayed for him absolutely drenched her.

"Yeah, I've said that a few times picturing it."

"Mmm, you fantasize about me?" The idea pleased her so much she felt giddy.

Coop's hand rose to her face, pushing aside a

curling tendril. She noted his fingers were not quite as steady as the pressure of his erection against her pelvis. "Taryn, I think about you, fantasize about you, dream about you."

She inhaled sharply. "You dream about me?"

"Uh-huh," he whispered, lowering his head to her neck, nuzzling the sensitive flesh below her ear.

Taryn tipped her head to the side for easier access and slid her palms inside his now open shirt. Should she confide her own dreams to him? Her heart quivered again and she decided against it. Tonight she would make his fantasies a reality as best she could. It was the least she could do to make up for the disastrous end to their day at the Faire.

When his mouth found hers again, she leaned into him, savoring the touch and softness of his lips for a moment before pulling away. "Why don't you go in the living room and I'll be right back?"

"Where are you going?"

"Just go sit for a minute, okay?"

He rubbed her shoulder. "Do you have to leave right now?" Looking down between them, he chuckled, thrusting his hips at her. "I'm as hard as a two-by-four."

"Hold that thought, Tiger," she whispered, molding his erection with the palm of her hand, groaning at the sexy feel of it. "I wanna see how much harder you can get."

Coop's sharply indrawn breath and pulse sent a rush of power through her. "What do you have in mind?"

She winked. "You'll see."

Scampering through the living room to the kitchen, she darted into the garage and rummaged through the saddlebags on her bike. Pulling her black leather chaps free, she shook them out and grinned. This was going to be fun.

She couldn't wait to see his face when she re-appeared. Taryn stripped off her jeans and T-shirt in the garage, doffing her bra after the briefest of hesitation. Coop's fantasy included only the chaps and she wanted to give him everything.

Her throat constricted slightly and her hands shook as she buckled the leather around her waist. What "everything" entailed she wasn't quite sure, but she felt free and daring with him. More adventurous than she had in the past few years. The recklessness that seemed always a part of her continued to thrive, but with Coop in the picture, it found new ways to express itself. Like stripping buck naked in her lit garage.

Looking over her shoulder at the houses across the street, she wondered if she saw a curtain twitch, then discounted it, deciding she didn't give a damn. Let the tongues wag.

Better yet, let Coop's tongue do the wagging. Her thighs clenched, rubbing against each other offering no relief. If anything, her decadent thoughts and leather dress only served to heighten her sexual awareness. Her fingers slipped between her legs and she moaned at the wetness she found. She was definitely ready for Coop's tongue, fingers and any other body part he cared to torment her with.

As long as they satisfied each other, his brand of torment could last all night long.

Easing open the door, she slipped inside, peeking around the corner. He wasn't where she left him. Damn, he hadn't gone home, had he?

"Coop, where are you?"

His muffled reply came from the bathroom and she relaxed.

Moving further into the living room, she quickly lit a few candles, turned down the lighting in the rest of the rooms, pulled up the special seduction playlist on her mp3 player and draped herself over the back of the couch, bare butt facing the hallway.

The position took her breath away, made her feel like a naughty schoolgirl and a wanton woman all rolled into one. Her heart pounded in time with her clit and her fingernails bit into damp palms.

"Hurry up, Coop," she pleaded, keeping her gaze on the bathroom door.

As if hearing her, the door opened and he walked out, stopping in the middle of the hall when he caught sight of her. Incredulity swept over his face, chased quickly away by a feral look of lust that made her even wetter.

"My God, Taryn."

She took his strangled voice and riveted gaze as positive signs. "Is this what you had in mind?" she purred, dropping one shoulder and spreading her legs further apart, offering him any and everything.

"Yeah," Coop rasped, moving behind her, bringing his hands slowly, almost reverently, down on her bare back.

Taryn shivered, wanting to close her eyes, but forcing them to remain open. Watching him look at her was nearly as much an aphrodisiac as having him inside her.

His fingers splayed widely on her hips, skirted the chaps and caressed the bare skin of her butt. When he knelt behind her, she twisted nearly double to keep his face in view. He looked like a man in the throw of a fantasy come to life. Exactly what she wanted. After all, fair was fair. He'd made so many of her fantasies real. More than real.

"Coop, tell me what you want me to do," she whispered, a bit uncertain in her role. Brazen bravado had gotten her this far, but she'd never been in a position like this before. She stifled a nervous giggle. Literally never a position like this. Her self-confidence seeped away with his continued silence and she half-rose, only to be stayed by the power of his hand at the small of her back.

"Don't move."

His warm breath wafted over her wet, open lips and she tensed, but remained belly flush to the brocade couch. The material felt shockingly cold to her overheated skin, her nerves raced and jangled and her entire concentration focused solely on Coop kneeling behind her.

Squeezing her eyes shut, she waited, silently urging him to touch her. Taste her. Fill her.

Please, please, please ran through her mind in a crashing litany so powerful her chest hurt from the building, near burning need.

Coop's fingers slid over her butt cheeks again before dropping to the insides of her thighs. Thumbs sweeping lazily over her skin, she felt him pulling her apart, felt the wetness of her desire clinging to her lips.

Please, please, please.

"Baby, you are so incredibly sexy, do you know that?"

A slight shake of her head was all she could manage.

"You are," he murmured.

Then he tried to drive her mad with one well-placed sweep of his tongue. Taryn moaned and dropped her head as far into the back of the couch as she could manage, leaning heavily on its stiff spine. Her knees shook continuously and the muscles in her thighs rippled in time with each hot swipe of Coop's talented mouth.

Please, please, please.

"Sweet, sweet baby."

Fisting one of the cocoa-brown throw pillows, she sucked in gasping breaths as she fought the orgasm he was giving her. She wanted it to last, wanted to ride it as long and hard as she could. The power of it was so strong, she knew she would have fallen if not for the couch and Coop's hands supporting her.

"Coop," she nearly-shouted as he slipped first one, then two fingers inside her slickness.

"Let it go, baby," he crooned softly, his talented hand slowly spearing her.

Her head thrashed and she groaned. "God, Coop."

Hand still bringing her to orgasmic pleasure,

he rose behind her and flattened his body against hers, the rough denim of his jeans scraping along the ultra-sensitive skin of her thighs, butt and back. "Now, baby," he whispered in her ear, kissing her neck. "Come for me."

And just like that, she did.

"Oh damn, oh damn, oh damn," she chanted, shaking hard. Grinding her hips back into his hand, Taryn gasped as each shock tightened her muscles around the fingers still inside her.

Coop pulled away before she was ready for him to, but she was too stunned by the depth of her climax to protest with more than a stifled moan.

"Just a sec, baby, I'm not going anywhere."

She relaxed, her hands releasing the chenille pillow, breathing still furious, heart beat still erratic.

It nearly stopped altogether when the tip of his cock spread her lips and slid smoothly in to the hilt with one stroke.

They groaned together and his hands tightened around her hips while hers found the pillow again.

"Yes," she hissed, hips twisting sinuously, loving the feel of him buried so deep within her. She felt every beat of his heart as he throbbed inside of her, could tell by the rapid pulse that he was as affected as she.

Coop withdrew slowly, gritting his teeth at her clinging tightness seeking to hold him within. He still couldn't believe she'd gone to this much trouble to make his fantasy come true.

He'd never had a partner so willing to please him. Sex had never been so mind-blowingly great as it was with this woman. Except he knew it wasn't just sex, there was too much feeling embroiled in it. Hopefully for both of them.

Looking down at her bare back bent over the couch, the creamy expanse of her skin draped only by the curls of her blond hair, he shuddered, fighting his orgasm.

Fighting the rush of love that swept over him.

A harsh groan escaped his clenched jaw. "Taryn" he rasped, the need to connect with her on more than just a physical level stronger than his need to come. And that was pretty damn strong.

A ripple of movement started around him again and he ran his hands up her back, tangling in her hair and tugging lightly until she raised her head, looking back over her shoulder at him.

Her eyes glistened with passion, her mouth open in a pleading moue. "Coop," she whispered. "Please." She shook her hips against him, still holding his gaze, and his heart, captive. "I need you."

"Ahhh," exploded from his mouth as he moved inside her, pulled back and surged forward again. And again.

His fingers fell from her hair, but she didn't look away. Breath quickening, he watched her orgasm on her face even as he felt it tighten around his cock. Her eyelids drooped, her mouth pursed and her nostrils flared. But still she held his eyes.

Coop swallowed hard, feeling as though she were invading his soul, demanding his all. He gave it, pistoning his hips faster and faster, riding through the condom-clutching strength of her climax, focusing on her face, her eyes, their pleasure.

"Now, Coop," she said huskily and he arched his back, slamming into her with a sharp, hard stroke until he came.

"This is getting to be familiar," Coop quipped as he buttoned his shirt. Too damn familiar and he wasn't sure he liked it.

Taryn, clad in a soft blue robe, wrapped her arms around his neck, laying her head on his shoulder. "What is?"

He pulled back slightly so he could see her face in the dim flicker of candlelight. Fitting his hand to the sweet curve of her jaw and cheek, he stroked her skin. "Leaving you."

She stilled then moved from him, away from his touch. Tightening the belt at her small waist, Taryn's silver-blue eyes studied him, but he didn't know what she was searching for. "You want to stay?"

Coop hesitated, sensing she stood at the edge. The wrong word, the wrong push could make her back away. But what were the right words? What did she want from him? "Do you want me to?"

The small frown melted from her face and

she laughed, again moving into his arms, squeezing him hard, her breasts pressed tightly to his chest. The position stirred more than just his arousal. Folding his arms around her, he closed his eyes and absorbed the feel of her.

His heart soared just from the simple pleasure of holding her. He wanted her to say yes, to ask him to share the night in her bed and her arms.

"Some night, yes, Coop, I want you to stay. But not tonight."

"Why not?"

Her lips feathered along his throat, teeth tugging lightly at his chest hair. "It's late and we both have to work in the morning. And don't you need to work on the Gleason proposal some more?"

Annoyance bit at him with the couple's name. They still hadn't signed. For some reason they were stalling and he'd be damned if he could figure out why. He didn't truly believe Monica and her thwarted seduction of him was behind the delay. He considered withdrawing from the negotiations, though, despite the prestige and importance an alliance with them offered. In his experience, difficult negotiations always indicated a difficult working relationship. But this one time, he was making an exception to his usual rule. He only hoped it didn't come around to bite him in the ass.

"Yeah," he conceded. "And I have a meeting with another client at two that I need to get some information together for."

"See, so it's better that you sleep at your

place and I sleep at mine."

It rankled. Dozens of rebuttals popped into his mind. He wanted to tell her that he could plug in his laptop anywhere and access his files, work from her house just as easily as his. His business was portable. But something was holding her back, and until he found out what it was, he would do his best not to push. Even if that meant going home.

With a sigh, he caressed her back, unwilling to release her soft form just yet. "Are you sure?"

"Yes," she murmured, petting his chest. "But I'll make it up to you. How about tomorrow for lunch, we have a picnic affair?"

"Affair?" he said lightly, trying to maintain the air of fun she obviously sought.

With a giggle, she swatted his arm. "I meant actual food, silly, but…" Rising on tiptoe, she kissed him with soft touches, melding their lips, breaking free, returning.

She was making him nuts. Not to mention hard.

Taryn's breathing changed, deepened and her hands slid down his chest to the waistband of his jeans, around and into his pockets where she gripped his butt through the denim.

"What was I saying?" she whispered.

"Hell if I know, but I like where you're going with this."

"You are a devil in jeans, Mr. Malone." With another bun-tingling squeeze she let go. "Tomorrow, I'll bring lunch and we'll have a nice picnic by the lake, how's that sound?"

It sounded hot and uncomfortable, but he'd

take time with her any way he could get it. Hundred degree heat, pesky mosquitoes, invasive ants and all. "Sounds great, baby."

Her smile lit up her face. "Great, I'll see you at eleven, then." She kissed him again before moving to the front door.

If he had a complex, he'd wonder at her motives behind the obvious dismissal, but the odd connection he had to her told him she desperately needed alone time. Could she have picked up on his deepening feelings for her? Was she running scared?

Coop swallowed hard as he stepped through the door. He would have to bide his time, be more careful with her. The last thing he wanted was to scare her away now.

Funny, he couldn't imagine Taryn scared, but looking up at him in the glow of her porch light, he clearly saw the worry lurking just beyond her blue eyes.

Leaning down, he dropped a feathery, comforting kiss on her lips. "Night, baby, sleep well."

"You, too, Coop."

With a final wave, he strode to his car and drove away, already plotting the events of the next day. Everything was going to be perfect.

The day was turning into a disaster and it was all Taryn's fault. Coop glared sourly at the contract in front of him and amended that thought. It was Taryn's absence that was the problem. Sleep had not come easily but when it did, she filled his night vision with sexy, come-hither looks and promises of long, passion-drenched lovemaking.

"Cooper, are you paying attention?" snapped Monica.

Ginger's stifled giggle brought his head up and he nodded. "Yes, of course, Mrs. Gleason. Just re-reading the numbers here with a bit of confusion."

"Why's that, son?" Troy asked.

"The consulting fee we agreed on seems to have been modified, as has the number of years for the length of the contract." His head hurt and he wondered what time it was. But he didn't dare check his watch. Again. "Would you care to explain?"

His tone must have held some of his frustration because Monica's perfectly penciled brow rose and Troy huffed, shifting in his seat.

"Well, son, our lawyer suggested the changes. He's looking out for our interests, you know. Just doing the job we pay him to do."

Coop didn't know whether to believe that or not. The phone at the reception desk rang and Ginger excused herself, leaving the glass door wide open. Little turkey probably wanted to eavesdrop in case she missed something juicy.

Juicy made him think of Taryn, splayed wantonly on the couch last night, open, eager, inviting.

Christ, she was going to kill him, he just knew it.

Concentrate, you idiot. He pushed the paper across the table. "Mr. Gleason, Troy, our agreement was for five years. I'll accept the lesser fee, but only if we sign for that length of time."

Where was she? Focusing on Monica, Troy and their ploys to work him was hard when she was always at the forefront of his mind. Damn woman played havoc with him. He smiled. He liked it.

"Cooper," Monica demanded again and he sighed.

"Yes?"

"I asked if you would like to join me for lunch to discuss it." She leaned back in her chair, crossing her legs so the hem of her pink skirt fell higher on her thighs.

Crap.

"Uh, actually, Monica …"

"Go on, son," Troy said heartily. "Can't join you myself, got some other errands to run that bore poor Monica to tears."

Oh hell, no. For one wild second he thought he'd said it aloud, because Monica's eyes widened and she suddenly sat up stiffly in the chair, head swiveling toward his door.

With both relief and trepidation, he watched as Taryn blithely breezed into the outer office carrying a picnic basket and offering Ginger a cheery hello. She winked at him through the glass partition of his doorway.

The sultry sound of her voice alone made his pants dance. Though it could have been the white, gauzy peasant skirt and blouse she wore, too. Déjà vu struck him and he swung his gaze to Monica, meeting her cold, hard glare head-on.

"You obviously have lunch plans, Mr. Malone." She rose, gathering her purse and looking down her nose at her husband. "Let's go, Troy."

Coop stood as well, frustration and anger surging at their manipulations. They were going to leave without signing again. His glance slid to Taryn and for one flitting moment, he wished she'd arrived ten minutes later. He could have begged off lunch with Monica and the Gleasons would have been none the wiser. Maybe they would have signed.

Taryn laughed at something Ginger said and the sound washed over him, flushing the thought away. No matter what glitches he encountered, he was glad she was in his life now.

Monica and Troy waited at the edge of his door, Monica staring at him with that damn eyebrow raised. Almost like a trained pet snake. He suppressed a laugh.

"Troy, if you see Ginger on your way out, she'll arrange another appointment at your convenience."

"Good, good," Troy stated, bustling his wife out of the office. "Hello again, Miss Kirkpatrick. You're looking lovely this morning."

Coop slowly walked to his doorway and propped a shoulder on the jamb, watching her charm Troy. Once more he studied Monica, not surprised to find her tense.

While it was not a good thing, Coop was

certain he'd find a way to appease her.

He hoped.

Chapter Ten

"Did the Gleasons sign?" Taryn asked, shifting the picnic basket as Coop pulled onto the winding road leading down to the lake.

When his fingers tightened to a white-knuckled grip on the steering wheel she winced and figured the answer was no. He confirmed her assumption a scant second later, his voice carefully even.

Reaching over, she squeezed his forearm, lingering along the muscled surface, nearly forgetting in the pleasure of the touch that she was supposed to be offering comfort. "You'll get it done, Coop, I just know it."

"Eventually, yes, I will."

Turning sideways in her seat, she directed him down the road to her favorite lakeside hideaway and contemplated this cocky side of him. She liked it.

Seeing it made her realize just how little she knew of Coop outside of the bedroom. Or the boardroom. Well, today she would rectify that. There would be no tumbling until they'd done some talking.

He stopped under the shade of a huge oak tree, killing the engine. "This is nice," he said.

"Yep. C'mon." She eased from the car, reaching in to grab the basket only to be foiled by his quick hands. The gentlemanly action warmed her and she smiled.

He grinned back at her across the leather seats. "Lead the way, Taryn."

At the front of the car, she held her hand out, curling her fingers around his when he took it, and tugged him down to a secluded patch of lush green grass and tall, well-canopied trees. Spreading the blanket she'd brought on the ground, she slipped off her shoes and sat.

Coop set the basket on one edge and eyed her curiously for a moment before grinning and shucking his suit jacket and tie. Hunkering down, he sat on the blanket close to her, almost touching, but not quite. Her mouth dried and her thighs clenched when he unfastened the top three buttons of his shirt, exposing his tan, muscular chest to her hungry gaze.

Talk first, sex later. Damn, that was going to be hard.

"So," her voice squeaked and she frowned, clamped her lips together and swallowed hard before trying again. "Tell me about you, Coop."

He looked startled. Draping his arms over his drawn knees he shrugged. "Not much to tell."

"'Course there is," she chided, scooting an inch or so closer.

His fingers slipped from his leg to the hem of her skirt, toying with the white lace. She unfolded her knees, bringing her thighs closer within his reach.

"What sort of hobbies do you have?"

Again his shoulders moved under his shirt, nearly distracting her from her vow of finding out what made this guy tick.

"None, really. No time for any, to tell you the truth."

His answer pulled her fully back to attention. "None? Surely there's something? Everyone has at least one thing that zings them."

"Zings them?" he teased, but she wasn't about to be swayed.

Frowning, she nodded. "Yeah. You know, for me it's my bike and shopping. What's your zing?"

"Huh." Coop's green gaze drifted over her face, down to her breasts and beyond, caressing her with his heated stare. "You make me zing. Hell, you make me so hard, I hurt."

A flush of pleased pride went through her, but she shook her head. "But what about something for just you? Do you play any sports or tinker with cars or—" She paused, trying to think of something uber-masculine, but drew a blank. "Anyway, something like that?"

"Why is this important?"

It was Taryn's turn to look over the calm surface of the water. How did she say it suddenly bothered her to be sleeping with a man who was barely more than a stranger? "It just is, Coop, okay? Humor me." Tipping her head back, she blinked into the sun. "Please?"

He chuckled and lay back on the blanket,

holding one arm up. "Come down here and we'll talk about it."

She knew that if she did that, talking would quickly segue into kissing, touching and making love. Not that she was opposed to that, quite the contrary. Already her body readied itself for him, anticipated his touch, being filled by him. But her mind rebelled, demanding coherent answers. For some reason that even went beyond her, she needed to know.

"If you don't have any hobbies, what's the one thing you wish you could do, but never have?"

He sighed and dropped his arm, folding his hands over his lean stomach, lips pursed. "Hmm, I'd have to say skydiving."

"What?" she nearly shrieked, totally surprised. "Why in the world would you want to do something so nutso?"

Coop's face closed and his shoulders tightened.

Damn her big mouth. Taryn could tell she'd hurt him with her idiotic reaction. God, hadn't she been exposed to that sort of crap when she was married to know better?

He started to sit up, but she pushed him back down gently, bending over him, searching his eyes. "I'm sorry."

His expression softened and he tucked a curl behind her ear only to have the hair fall right back out. "It's okay," he murmured. "I've always wanted to fly. Since I was a little kid. Built model airplanes by the dozen, decorated my room in posters of air force planes and even applied to the academy."

"Why didn't you go?"

"Dad died and Mom nearly fell apart. She needed me and I couldn't leave her."

"Okay, so how does flying a plane translate into hurling yourself from a plane with only a parachute to save you? I mean, really Coop, I've got bras with cups bigger than those parachutes."

He laughed, reached behind her head and hauled her down to his chest, swallowing her indignant protest as he kissed her.

Pulling back, his green gaze searched hers and she had a hard time concentrating on anything but his taste, which still lingered on her tongue.

"Freedom," he whispered.

"To do what?"

A flush crept up his neck. "To just be. Freedom to be just me. Not a son, not a friend, not an employer, just me."

Taryn's breath caught. She understood that concept so well it scared her. It was how she felt about the bike. What started out as a rebellion against all things "establishment" and what her ex represented, quickly became an extension of herself. When on her bike, she truly felt like she was flying. In total and complete control.

Herself.

Perhaps she and Coop were more alike than she ever imagined.

No. He couldn't be, he mustn't be. Coop was a white-hot affair and nothing more.

Then why the questions? She didn't have an

answer, not even the inkling of one and that scared the hell out of her. She refused to believe for one minute that she could be entertaining the idea of anything more than the fun tumble in bed Coop was.

It wasn't time. He couldn't be the one. He wasn't the one.

Was he?

Desperate to squelch the rampant thoughts, Taryn leaned over him and traced his soft lips with her finger, losing herself in him. His mouth parted and he nipped at her finger, but she shook her head.

"Let me touch you," she said.

He nodded, propping his hands behind his head. "I'm all yours, baby."

Hand trembling again, she let her fingers drift over the rough angles of his jaw, feeling the bristle of his five o'clock shadow starting already. So masculine, strong. Everything she'd always dreamed he was. And so much more.

"Coop," she whispered, moving closer, aching to feel him, to taste him.

Apparently he felt the same because his hands came free and he cupped her shoulders, finding her mouth in a burning kiss that shook her to her toes. When he took control and slid her over his body, Taryn didn't resist, but reveled in the feeling. The exhilaration.

Bracing her hands over his chest, she dug her fingers into his pecs as he smoothed his palms up the back of her thighs, lifting her skirt as he did so.

"Do you know how much I want you,

Taryn?" he rasped.

She moved sinuously against his hard-on, riding the ridge with small, delicate movements that threatened to incinerate them both. "Not as much as I want you," she replied.

With one quick roll, he had her beneath him, his nimble fingers pulled her skirt up and his pants down. When he tugged a condom from his pocket, she plucked the latex covering from his hands, knelt between his outstretched legs and rolled it on. After several long, slow swipes of her tongue, of course.

"Witch," he breathed once she'd protected him.

"I know."

Taryn's breath hissed out in an erotic moan of longing as she straddled him, sinking down onto his hard, hot erection.

Coop's reaction was no less wild. He bucked beneath her, driving himself home as far as he could.

Together they moved and swayed, battling for dominance until Taryn arched her back, hands tangled in her own hair, trying to maintain some semblance of control, but it was a useless effort as Coop's strong movements within her set off an orgasm. Crying out his name, she slumped forward, head to his chest, hips still writing on him.

Coop groaned and grabbed her butt, his fingers holding her tightly against him as he, too, came.

Long, quiet minutes passed without either one of them moving. Taryn didn't want to lose

the incredible joy she found just from touching
him and he seemed as content to stroke her skin,
hold her in his arms. Besides, she doubted rather
seriously she would be able to move for a week.
Finally, the heat of the sun and the grass poking
through the blanket forced her hand and she
lifted away from him, offering a wobbly grin.
"You are one incredible man, Cooper Malone."

He shook his head, his fingers combing
through her hair, his face a mix of sated pleasure
and tender wonderment. "No, baby, you are the
incredible one. Never before, Taryn."

The words made her heart swell even as her
head screamed a warning. Taryn hovered,
wondering what the hell to do. The sound of an
approaching car spurred her to move off of him,
even if she was gasping at the loss of his length
sliding from her.

"Curses," he laughed then removed the
condom and wrapped it in one of the napkins
she'd brought. "Good thing we're both so well-
prepared."

He winked and pulled up his pants just as the
car crested the hill. Though she knew they were
well-hidden from any onlookers curiosity, Taryn
scrambled to put her skirt back into place and
tug on the thong panties that somehow ended up
hooked on the picnic basket.

She checked her watch. "It's nearly two,
Coop. I guess we don't have time to eat."

His hand slid over her hip, darting between
her legs before she slapped him away with a
breathless laugh.

"Nope, more's the pity. My mouth was

watering at the thought of Taryn pie."

She rolled her eyes. "Neanderthal."

"Horny man who knows what he likes," he corrected her.

"Oh, excuse me, horny man." Taryn stood on knees that still shook. There was no denying Coop's effect on her as a sexual being. Never in her life had she experienced the depth of passion and fulfillment as she did at his hands. And other body parts. Still playing the ostrich, she preferred to bury her head and ignore all but the flush of a satisfying orgasm. "We need to go. I've got to get to the opera and I'm sure you have some paperwork at the office to work on."

Coop's gaze narrowed on her before he stood and scooped up the blanket. When she would have lifted the basket, he caught her hand. "Baby, are you okay? I didn't hurt you, did I?"

The worry in his voice tore at her heart and her tenuous emotional control teetered a bit more. "Oh, no, Coop, you didn't. It was wonderful."

As always.

"I just don't want you to be so late getting back to work that Ginger gives you a hard time."

For a wild moment, she thought he would call her on the lie, but he didn't. Instead, he caressed her cheek with his thumb, then kissed her lips with such soft gentleness it nearly undid her. "Okay, baby. But you're the one who gives me the hard time, not Ginger."

With a grin, he took the basket and wrapped his hand around her free one. "I guess we should go. I'd rather spend the day here with you."

So would she and that scared the hell out of her.

"Boss, where the heck have you been? Mr. Tottleston waited nearly thirty minutes. And why didn't you answer your cell? I called a dozen times at least. He was pissed when he left!"

Ginger's tirade effectively destroyed the after-incredible-sex euphoria Coop had been riding.

Tottleson. He'd completely forgotten his two o'clock meeting. Bile rose in his suddenly too dry throat and his hands fisted at his side. He never forgot meetings, never forgot clients, never put work second. *Never before Taryn.*

"Coop?" The hesitant voice came from Taryn and he schooled his features best he could before looking at her. Giving her a tight smile, he shook his head and glanced at Ginger.

"Did you reschedule him?"

Ginger's wide-eyed gaze was fastened on his knees and he resisted the urge to look down, fairly certain that despite the blanket, he would find bits of grass and dust on his slacks. Clear evidence of his illicit afternoon activities.

Damned if he didn't feel like a six year old in trouble with the teacher.

"Ginger," he snapped.

Her head whipped up.

"Coop." Taryn spoke again, this time her voice held more insistence, more demand for his attention.

Still reeling from his unusual lack of responsibility, Coop avoided her gaze. "I'm sorry, Taryn, but I've got to take care of this. Give me a minute, okay?"

A low hum issued from her general direction and he took it as assent, returning his attention to Ginger. "Did you give him a new time?"

"No," she said, swallowing hard. "He, uh... he didn't want one. Said he wanted to talk to you personally."

"Damn," he muttered. Loosening the buttons he'd re-fastened only in the parking garage, he stalked toward his office. "Get him on the phone."

"Yes, sir."

Coop sank into his chair and wiped a hand over his face, exhaling loudly. How the hell had this happened?

"Coop?"

Lips pressed into a grim line, he looked up, meeting Taryn's worried gaze. "Yeah?"

Shifting on her strappy heels, she clicked her bronzed nails against the glass of his door and nibbled her bottom lip.

"I'm sorry about your appointment."

Coop nodded, looking at the console. "Thanks." He wanted to tell her it wasn't her fault, that this sort of stuff happened. Problem was, it didn't. Not to him. Ever.

Not before Taryn.

The phone buzzed and he reached for the

handset as he looked at her. "I'll call you later tonight, okay?"

"Sure," she mumbled, watching him with a hooded gaze. "Sure, tonight. Bye."

With a half-hearted wave, she turned on her heel and walked out, shoulders and head high and stiff. Coop, torn between the urge to run after her and the need to soothe his client, let slip a vicious curse and lifted the ringing phone, bracing himself for the man's well-deserved tirade.

Coop wasn't going to call. Taryn hugged her tiger-striped chenille pillow closer to her chest and stared at her phone. She punched the home button then glared at the cell as it flashed the time at her. Sixteen past midnight.

He wasn't calling.

Not that she blamed him. The look on his face when he'd realized he'd missed the appointment still made her stomach clench and her eyes burn. The ridiculous reaction only made her more emotional.

He'd forgotten her the minute business came back to call. Just like her ex.

But her heart whispered unfair. She'd been the one to tempt and keep him at the lake, cuddling and kissing after making love. It was her fault and she would take responsibility for it.

He was right not to call, though it rankled just a little bit. Smacked of manipulation, a trait she absolutely detested. Again her heart battled her mind, insisting Coop wouldn't treat her that way.

She could call him... The phone sat next to her on the couch, mostly hidden by Velvet's fur as she lay wrapped around it. Reaching out for it, Taryn dug her fingers into Velvet's softness instead, sighing.

It was too late. They both needed to work. She needed to sleep. If only her mind would shut down. The scene at the lake spun over and over in her head. What could she have done differently? What would she have done differently?

The bruising truth was nothing. Taryn knew she wouldn't give up a minute of being touched and loved by Coop, no matter what it cost. She had every faith that he would take care of this and in the morning all would be right with them.

He'd call her tomorrow. She yawned and stretched her legs out, displacing both the cat and the phone. Laying her head on the pillow, she closed her eyes, promising herself she'd get up and go to bed in just a minute.

"Coop?" Taryn stood in his office, listening to the jangle of the phones, wondering why neither he nor Ginger answered them.

Picking up the handset, she punched one of the flashing buttons and said hello only to be waylaid by a screaming female voice which sounded remarkably like Monica Gleason. Taryn slammed the receiver back down.

The phone rang again and she stared at it like it was a venomous snake, but when no one appeared to answer it again, she picked it up.

When she told the caller Coop wasn't around, he became very disgruntled and demanded she take a message. Jotting the information down, Taryn hung up the phone and backed away. She wasn't picking it up again.

"Coop?" she yelled louder.

A muffled shout answered her from the foyer and she turned, finding him seated on the outer couch, hands folded in his lap, eyes burning with suppressed anger, mouth slammed into a hard, tight line.

"I can't believe what you caused," he accused.

"Huh?"

"The lake, Taryn. Don't play innocent. I doubt there's an innocent bone in your delectable body." He shook his head.

"Hey," she protested, moving forward, standing in front of him, hands propped on her hips. "You were just as involved as I was, bucko. Just as in as I was."

His face changed, sliding from angry to sensual in the whiff of a breath. "Yeah, I was in, alright. In your luscious, tight body."

Her apprehension melted and she flicked open her blouse. "Did you like it?"

"Hell, yeah, baby." Coop stood, his green gaze fixed on the cleavage she uncovered. "I liked it a lot."

"How about some more?" she purred, swaying toward him, one hand sliding down his chest, hovering at his waistband.

His fingers clamped down over hers. "No,"

he said harshly. "I think you've done enough damage."

Taryn's eyes flicked open, staring at the dawn-lit dust motes of her living room. Her head hurt, her back hurt and Velvet's sharp little claws were kneading her thigh.

Moving the cat off, Taryn stretched, popping her spine and hips, relieving the pressure. Good, her back felt better. And now that the little minx wasn't using her for a scratching post, her leg felt better. But the pounding continued.

It took a second for her sleep-sedated mind to realize the noise was coming from the door and not her head. Sitting up, she looked warily in the direction of the foyer, frowning when she made out Coop's voice over his repeated thumps.

That woke her up like nothing else. He was supposed to call, not come over. And why hadn't he called, anyway?

"Just a minute," she yelled, throwing back the covers and nearly tumbling to the floor in her haste to get to the door. Shrugging into her robe, she grimaced at her reflection in the mirror, swiping her fingers through her sleep-tousled hair.

"Damn." Sticking her head around the corner of the doorjamb, she eyed the bathroom. Did she have time? Taryn cupped her hand and exhaled sharply, sniffing. Definitely needed some mouthwash. "Hang on, Coop, be there in a sec."

His muffled agreement filtered through the door and she skidded across the hallway, downed a mouthful of fresh mint tastiness and ran the brush through her hair at the same time.

She was getting better a multi-tasking.

Thirty seconds later, she sped to the front door and opened it, leaning casually against the wood. "Morning," she murmured, drinking him in. Coop was dressed in tight jeans, a forest green henley that didn't bare enough of his yummy chest and running shoes. He also wore a sinful grin that made her toes curl against the hardwood floor.

"Hey, beautiful." Shifting on the porch, he met her eyes, a rueful look of apology clear in his. "I'm sorry about last night."

Just like that, whatever hint of agitation she may have felt dissipated. "Hey yourself. Don't worry about it. Come in?"

"Yeah, but I'll wait in the living room while you get dressed." He stepped inside, catching her around the waist and kissing her with a long, shiver-inducing motion that made her entire morning brighter.

"Dressed for what?" she managed when he released her.

Coop's wink and devious smile did little to dampen her mood. He shut the door, turned her and lightly pushed her in the direction of her bedroom. "Just throw on some jeans and a comfortable shirt. Hurry up, okay?"

Taryn looked over her shoulder at him, wondering at this odd, mischievous mood. It seemed totally out of character for him. But maybe it wasn't...

The thrill of discovering yet another facet to this man had her dressed and ready in record time. Fifteen minutes from naked and barely brushed to dressed and presentable. A new record, if she did say so herself.

With measured calm, belied by the racing of her heart, she strolled back to the living room where he sat on her couch. Velvet lay shamelessly sprawled over his lap, tummy up and eyes closed in utter contentment as he rubbed her belly. Taryn froze in surprise. Velvet never, ever let a man touch her.

Until Coop.

Lots of things had changed since this man had entered her life. And Taryn found herself alternately fascinated and fearful. The potential for hurt was alarming, but the pleasure was even greater. All she had to do was stay focused on the fun. Totally doable. She hoped.

"Okay, Tiger, what's on the docket for today and why on earth does it have to start at 6 o'clock in the morning?"

Coop's hand slid over Velvet's fur once more before he displaced her and stood. "Early morning air is the best for what I have in mind."

"Mmm, now I like the sound of that." With a wink, she picked up her purse. "I'm all yours."

He grinned, rubbing his hands together as he walked toward her. "Great, get ready, Taryn, cause we're going skydiving."

"Huh?" She shook her head positive she'd misheard. He did not just say... "Skydiving?"

"Yep, I found this really cool place through a friend of mine. He says it's rocking and I need to try it."

"Uh, okay, so have fun." Setting her purse back on the table, she crossed her arms. "This chick is not going."

His face fell, making her feel like she'd run over a furry forest critter with her bike. "I bought two passes, Taryn. One for each of us."

"I appreciate the thought Coop, but why on earth would you do that without asking me first? I mean, skydiving is not exactly primo date material."

"You're an adventurous woman, Taryn. I figured this would be right up your alley." Holding up the colorful brochure he smiled again. "Come on, please? For me?"

"Oh, that is so low." Taryn bit her lip, wondering if insanity ran in her family, because she was actually considering it. "I don't know, Coop."

"Great," he said, moving forward. Picking up her purse, he hooked her around the waist and hustled her out the door.

With a long sigh, she locked up, praying it wasn't for the last time. She really had no desire to die today. Squinting up into the already warm Texas morning, she couldn't deny the adrenaline coursing through her. Whether it was the thought of throwing herself out of an airplane or Coop's company, she wasn't entirely sure.

"You're quiet," he said, backing out of the driveway and heading out of the cul-de-sac.

"Mentally preparing my will," she quipped. "Got any paper handy?"

He laughed. "It won't be bad, I promise. Where's your sense of adventure?"

"At home in bed, where I should be."

"This from a woman who rides a Harley? You surprise me."

"Keep in mind a bike stays on the ground, Coop. It doesn't entail lots of big empty air, a thin piece of fabric and a very, very hard ground."

He turned off the highway and down a bumpy road that led to a wide field. "Well hell, when you put it that way ..."

"Changing your mind?" she asked eagerly.

"Nah, but I'll tell you what. You can haunt me all you want if you die. How's that?"

"Just swell, bucko." She shook her head, looking around at the various cars and planes jammed around a sleek, white hanger. "Don't think I won't do it, either."

Forty-five minutes later, head buzzing with all the instructions imparted by the jump guide, Taryn couldn't believe she was climbing into the plane behind Coop. The only reason she'd agreed was because it would be a tandem jump. She'd be safely strapped to the instructor as they fell through air and space to the ground. It would be his responsibility to pull the chute cord at the right time and get them safely down.

With a groan, she slumped into a seat and tried to glare at Coop, but his enthusiasm and grin made it damn difficult. He looked like a kid in a Norman Rockwell Christmas painting: wide-eyed, excited and so darn cute it made her heart flutter.

The engines revved and she buckled in, resigned to doing the deed. Sneaking a glance at Coop again, she couldn't hide her own smile.

He was practically bouncing in his seat.

"Isn't this great?" he asked.

"Yeah," she said softly, realizing that making him happy made her happy. Her brow furrowed. Hmm, was that a good thing?

"Thank you for coming with me, Taryn," he said loudly to be heard over the roar of the plane and she nodded, reaching over to take his hand. They stayed that way until the two instructors stood and signaled them forward, indicating they'd entered the drop zone.

"Ready, baby?" Coop asked.

Palms sweaty, heart racing and tummy faintly rebellious, she wanted to shake her head, but she wasn't a coward. Not anymore. She'd promised him she would do this and she would keep her word.

Even if it killed her.

Oh, God.

The instructor winked and gave her the thumbs up before spinning her around and strapping her into the intricate harness attached to his jump suit. Sliding the goggles over her eyes, she closed them, praying this would go quickly. A loud buzz sounded in the cabin and her eyes snapped wide, focusing on the two light bulbs above the now-open cabin door. In less time than she was prepared for, the lights switched from red to green. Her muscles tensed in anticipation and she waited for the handler's signal, a light touch to her right shoulder.

When it came, she drew in a deep breath, bent her knees and found herself screaming thirteen thousand feet to the ground. With effort, she closed her mouth, forced her eyes to remain open and on the fast-approaching field below and prayed. Hard. Suddenly the momentum shifted, the free-fall taking on a more controlled feeling. Taryn relaxed only minutely, but enough to absorb the incredible feeling of flying, of coursing through the air.

Wow.

Squinting at the altimeter strapped around her wrist, she watched it crank backward, the dial spinning madly as they descended.

Craning her head as best she could around her instructor's chest, she searched for Coop, finding them also gliding smoothly down. The look on his face was worth every second of the fearful agony she'd gone through. Christmas, Halloween and his birthday, all rolled into one. Though, she thought he looked like he might toss his cookies at any minute.

The instructor tapped her again and she raised her hands, hooking them around the nylon harness and nodded, preparing herself to be jerked upward when he released the chute. He'd offered to let her steer or pull the cord, but she'd declined, not quite that ready to take her own life in her hands. The tug and jerk wasn't nearly as bad as she'd imagined it would be. A bit painful on the neck, but not too bad.

They floated down, landing gently among the tall grasses of the field adjacent the airstrip. After being unbuckled, she looked up, shading her eyes to watch as Coop came down.

No sooner were his own straps free than he was at her side.

"So? What did you think?"

Trying to gauge his reaction, she smiled. "It was something. What about you?"

With a whoop and a wild chuckle, he grabbed her, spinning her around in circles. "I think we're freakin' nuts!"

She laughed, latching onto his neck. "Yeah, I'd agree. Uh, Coop?"

"Yeah, baby?" He set her down, kissing her lips with quick, firm pressure.

"We are not doing this again."

Chapter Eleven

"That was incredible," Coop said on the way back to Taryn's house. The blood still pumped through him with wild speed.

"Uh-huh."

He slanted her a glance. "What, you didn't like it?"

"It was...interesting."

He laughed, easily reading between her meager lines. "Interesting, huh?"

"Yep. I meant it, Coop, no way will you get me back up there. I don't know what I was thinking. No one is going to believe I did this."

Coop shot her a disbelieving look. "Really? That surprises me. Seems like it would be something right up your alley."

"I'm adventurous, yes, suicidal, no." The amusement in her tone took the edge off her words.

"Then why did you do it?"

A long silence filled the car as it ate up the miles to her house. "Taryn?"

She sighed. "I don't know."

Despite her spontaneous attitude, Coop's instincts told him she knew perfectly well why she'd gone up with him. She just wasn't telling.

The cautious optimistic in him flared to life.

"Well, no matter why, I'm glad you did."

"Have you satisfied your flying desires now, Coop?"

"Somewhat. It may not be the culmination of all my dreams, but it's a good start." He slid his hand over the console, pleased when her fingers entwined with his. "I have to tell you, Taryn, being with you has changed me. In a good way."

She squeezed his hand. "I'm glad. I'd hate to be a bad influence," she said half-teasingly.

His mind flashed back to yesterday's missed appointment. An aberration he wouldn't repeat. The rest of his time with her had been golden. The stuff bachelors dreaded because it made them think of gold bands, wedding singers and forever.

He swallowed hard, jerking the car back into his own lane.

"Hey, just because you pay for the middle doesn't mean you get to drive in it," Taryn said reproachfully. "Are you okay?"

Marriage. That was serious. Damn serious. Coop's throat tightened and he looked at her. "I'm fine," he rasped. She was beautiful, witty, articulate. Hell, she was a damn personals ad come to life. Into his life. "Just thinking."

"Must have been some heavy thoughts. Care to share?"

Coop needed a lot more time to process the

impossible thoughts swirling in his mind. "Random stuff."

Taryn's silent perusal made him damn glad to see the turnoff for her house. She didn't speak until he'd pulled into the drive and killed the engine.

"Are you all right? Really, don't give me any lines, okay?"

"Yeah, I'm good." He looked at her, seeing the doubt in her face, knowing she had good reason for those feelings. But he needed to think, needed to focus. "Look, I'll call you later, okay?"

Her brows knitted together as she shoved open her door. With a small, albeit forced, chuckle, she got out. Bending down, one hand on the door, the other over her head, she studied him again. "Last time you said you'd call, you didn't. This isn't baseball, Coop."

He winced. "What's that mean?"

"It's not three strikes and you're out. You only get two with me. When you're done thinking, call me. Doesn't matter what time it is."

With a nod and smile of his own, he started the car again. "I will. Promise."

"Great. Later." Slamming the door shut, she stepped away and he backed out of the drive, heading for the office.

Marriage. What the hell was he thinking? He'd never intended for their affair, as satisfying as anything he'd ever experienced, to become this entangled. This serious.

Despite her stellar performance at the

Gleason's dinner party, she was the antithesis of the corporate wife. She didn't fit. But she had. And she could. But she wasn't happy doing it.

Coop stomped into his office, bypassing Ginger without even a nod. Shucking his jacket, he slumped into his chair, spun around and stared sightlessly at the fast-moving freeway traffic outside his window.

"Boss? You okay?"

He sighed. Images of Taryn flashed through his mind, from silly to sensual and every facet in between. Each one tugged at his heart and he groaned, dropping his head in his hands.

"Boss!" With a gasp and quick footsteps, Ginger skirted his desk and shoved at his shoulder.

"What?" he growled.

"Are you okay?"

"Why does everyone keep asking me that?" he grumbled.

She frowned, stepping back. "Maybe because you stormed in here like a wet cat, you've got a look on your face like you lost every deal on the books and you haven't even asked about the Taylor account. So, what's going on?"

Could he tell her? Would she laugh? It really didn't matter. Besides Chris, her older brother, Ginger was the only other person who really knew him. Knew his past.

"Sit down, Ginger."

He swung around as she moved to the chair fronting his desk. "Spill it, Coop. What's going on?"

The worry on her face niggled at his

conscience and he sighed heavily. "It's Taryn."

His young friend's expression eased. "Well thank heavens for that. I thought it was serious."

"It is serious, Ginger. Too serious. And that's the problem."

"Huh? Too serious? Coop, what are you talking about?"

"I...damn it." Rubbing his hand over his face, he stared at her through suddenly bleary eyes. "I think I love her."

Ginger clapped and squealed. "But that's wonderful. It's about time. Oh, we're going to have a wedding."

"No," he cut in forcefully.

"No?" Ginger stared at him, brown eyes narrow and thoughtful. "Wait a sec, did you say loving her is a problem?"

"Yes."

"Why?"

Yeah, why? "It just is."

She shook her head, blond hair moving wildly, lips flattened in a tight line. "You are not getting off that easily, Cooper Malone. In all the years I've known you, I've never heard you mention the L word. Why is it a problem?"

Coop shoved his chair back and stood, pushing his hands deep in his pockets and turning to face the window again. "She's different."

"Yes, she is."

"She's not corporate wife material. She could be a detriment instead of an asset." There, he spit it out. Said the one thing that hounded his mind since he realized how he might feel for her. Might feel. "And this could just be lust, you know. It might not even be the other thing."

Ginger's prolonged silence finally got to him and he looked over his shoulder, surprised to find her standing. She had a small smile on her face and she was nodding.

Nodding?

"What?" he asked, stupefied.

"You are absolutely correct, Coop. She is all wrong for you." She breathed deeply, her smile widening. "I am so glad you realized that now. I didn't know how I was going to talk to you about it."

"Wrong for me?"

"Oh, yes, definitely. I mean, look at yesterday's snafu. Would have never happened if you hadn't been with her."

He scowled, hands coming out of his pockets. "I'm a grown man, Ginger, old enough to remember my own schedule. She had nothing to do with it."

"Right," Ginger nodded sagely, obviously not believing a word of his denial. "However, she does dress herself. Have you seen those clothes? Some portion of her is bare at all times. Not exactly the best impression to make on a client, is it?"

"To hell with some narrow-minded idiot's view, she's beautiful. She has style."

"Okay, what about—"

"Not to mention," Coop raised his voice to be heard over her. "She's intelligent and charming. A wiz at making people comfortable and relaxed. Her people skills are phenomenal.

She had them all eating out of her hand at the Gleason's house party." He glared at his secretary. "She can do whatever she puts her mind to."

"Then why is she wrong for you?"

He stilled. Why was she wrong for him? He sank back into his chair, staring up at a now-smiling Ginger. "I can't love her, Ginger."

"Why not?"

With a deeply sucked in breath, Coop spilled his fear. "What if she doesn't love me back?"

"Oh, Coop." Ginger raced around the desk, throwing her arms around him and hugging him tightly. "She adores you. It's in her eyes every time she looks at you."

"She said it was an affair of convenience," he rasped, still reeling from the revelation.

Love.

"It may have started that way, but it's changed. For both of you."

He shook his head. "I don't know, Ginger, she's pretty damn skittish. She hated being at the Gleason's. Said it was too much of her past come back to life. That she wasn't that person anymore. Not to mention her ex was a jerk and I'm afraid I remind her too much of him."

"Baloney. You are unique, Coop, and Taryn knows it. You just might need a bit of help proving it to her."

He sighed, totally at a loss. "What do I do now?"

"What do you want? I mean, really, really want?"

"I—"

"Wait," Ginger ordered imperiously. "Don't answer that just yet. Take the rest of the day, think about it and we'll talk some more tomorrow."

"I'm supposed to call her tonight," he said, feeling like a thirteen-year-old asking his older sister for dating advice. Except Ginger was his best friend's baby sister. But if she had the answers, right now he'd gladly take them, because God knew he didn't have a freaking clue.

"Call her. Make small talk. Ask her to lunch tomorrow. You're meeting with the Taylors, she can meet you at the restaurant."

Coop looked down at his planner, mind once again whirling, heart thumping. "How do I know this is real?"

Ginger smiled almost pityingly. "What's the first thing you think of in the morning?"

The question took him unawares and he opened his mouth to automatically answer work … except he suddenly realized that wasn't true. He gulped. "Taryn."

"And the last thing?"

"Taryn," he whispered hoarsely, seeing what she was driving at. "But that doesn't mean anything. She's incredible, both in bed and out."

Ginger winced, clapping her hands over her ears. "Coop!" she wailed.

"Sorry," he muttered.

She dropped her hands. "What's wrong now?"

"How do you know that just because I think of her means I'm in love with her?"

"God, you are such an idiot." Ginger stuck her tongue out at him before grinning. "Love is different for everyone, Coop. Some people know right away they're fated to be together, others it takes years to figure out. Most people fall somewhere in the middle. The only true thing to know about love is that there are no guarantees. She might be your one, your true love, but unless you try, you'll never know."

"No offense, Ginger, but this sucks."

She laughed. "Yeah, this part usually does. Once you realize you're in love with someone, the doubt and fear sets in until you hear the same from them. Rejection hurts, Coop. But a life without loving, without taking the risk, is no life at all."

He stared at her, somewhat bemused that this little girl, this sprite he'd watched grow from skinned-knee tomboy to very adult woman, sounded so mature. So knowledgeable.

"So, what are you going to do, Coop?"

Panic set in again. "I don't know. What do you think I should do?"

Ginger rolled her eyes. "You should feel her out. Invite her to lunch tomorrow, see how she does. If she's comfortable with the clients then step it up. Slowly but surely bring her into your world as much as you can. She'll see that she can belong."

"Slow and easy, yeah, that could work."

She nodded. "Trust me on this one."

"Okay, I'll ask her tonight."

For the second night in a row, Taryn found herself staring at her cell, willing it to ring. Fortunately, it was only a little after seven, nowhere near midnight. Yet.

Velvet lay draped over her shoulders, purring softly, occasionally swiping a rough-tongued kiss along Taryn's cheek.

"He'll call," she told the cat.

Velvet rumbled and shifted, batting at a stray curl.

"Yeah, I wonder what that was all about, too."

Taryn shifted on the couch, staring at the peach scented candlelight flickering from the coffee table. What put him in such a deep mood this afternoon?

His sudden shift from adrenaline-junkie to judge-somber had taken her by surprise. And had her worried.

Despite her claim that he wouldn't get another chance should he fail to call tonight, Taryn knew she couldn't let it go just like that.

What they had was too good, too hot, to let slip away just because he was phone-deficient.

She picked up the portable and shook it. "Ring, damn you."

Her small shriek when it did sent Velvet flying from her shoulders with a hiss and pointed flounce of her tail.

Coop's face smiled at her from the screen. Taryn took a deep breath, let it ring again, pushed the talk button and said hello as casually as she could.

"Hi." His voice flowed like mellow wine over her frazzled nerves and she smiled, sinking back onto the couch, crossing her feet and getting comfortable.

"So, okay, what's up? How was the rest of your day?"

"Small talk, Taryn? Don't you think we're a bit past that?"

"Probably. Feel like talking now?"

He sighed. "Yeah, sorry about that."

"Don't apologize, Coop. We all need our space."

"Space, huh? Funny, that's not what I was thinking about. Anything but, to tell you the truth."

"Mmm, that sounds promising." Taryn wrinkled her nose, one hand resting lightly on her stomach, making small circles with her forefinger. "You do know the opposite of space is proximity, don't you?"

"Is it?" Coop's voice deepened and she was pretty sure he was imagining just how close two people could get. But just in case...

"Oh, yeah. Body-to-body close. Thigh-to-thigh, chest-to-chest and every part in between." Her hand slid a bit lower, hovering at the waistband of her red lace panties. The ones she'd put on for just this phone call.

"Are you trying to seduce me over the phone?" he rasped.

"Yes," she whispered, fingers lightly scraping over her carefully trimmed pubic hair with just enough pressure to start her juices flowing. "Is it working?"

"Hell, yeah."

"Good."

Fabric rustled from his end and he grunted softly.

"What are you doing?" she asked.

"Getting more comfortable."

Images of Coop sprawled naked and glorious in his hard, erect state taunted her. Damn, she wished he was waiting in her bed. "Tell me."

"Tell you what?"

She hesitated, a bit unsure. She'd never had phone sex before. Her fingertips smoothed over her clit. "Tell me where you are." Somehow the words didn't sound at all silly, instead full of seductive pleading.

"In my bed. Where are you?"

"Living room. On the couch." She wiggled her hips, tossing the panties to the floor and pulling the chenille throw over her mostly naked body.

"What are you wearing?" he asked, voice pitched just a bit lower, raspier than before.

"Nothing."

He groaned. "Me, either."

"Coop." His named whispered from her as she slid one leg to the floor, the other climbing the back of the couch.

"I know, baby. I know." The silence between them was broken only by the soft sound of flesh stroking flesh. "This isn't why I called," he gritted out.

"Why later," she murmured, fingers finding

and giving exquisite, familiar pleasure. "Talk to me now. Tell me what you're doing."

Closing her eyes, Taryn listened as he described how his hand felt sliding over his hard cock, how much he wished it was her hand, her mouth, her body instead.

When he started telling her how much he wanted her again, reminding her of their passionate interludes, of how he'd had her bent over the couch, she gasped and moved her hand faster, gripped the phone tight.

"Coop, Coop," she moaned, her orgasm very close.

"Do it, baby, let me hear you come." His voice was thick with need and she gave it to him, writhing on the couch, crying out with the wave of pleasure that overtook her.

Dimly in the swirled recesses of her mind, she heard him shout her name as he, too, came.

Hearing his orgasm had sent another, powerful shockwave through her, setting off smaller pleasure bursts.

Her whole body shook and a wide smile curved her lips. Withdrawing her hand, she closed her legs, careful not to put any pressure on her ultra-sensitive mound and adjusted the phone. "Wow, that was fun," she murmured.

"I was just about to say the same thing." He gave a sudden, sharp crack of laughter. "I find myself doing the most amazing things around you."

Taryn was glad he couldn't see the blush she felt sweeping over her body. "There are first times for everything. I wish you'd been here in person, but phone sex will do in a pinch."

"It'd have to be a damn big pinch, baby. I prefer you, the real woman."

"Hey, it sounded like you were having fun."

"I did, but listening to you, picturing you doing that, drives me crazy. I think I've found another fantasy you can fulfill."

Her breath caught. "What?"

He chuckled softly. "I want to watch you do it in person. Just for me, baby."

"Oh, Coop." The sexy thought nearly had her hand back between her legs, but she resisted. For now.

"Yeah, I know." He cleared his throat. "Uh, an unfortunate side effect of our joint fun happens to be puddling on my stomach. I guess I'd better jump in the shower."

Taryn giggled. "I suppose I should, too." With a sigh, she tossed the coverlet off and sat up. "Hey, wait a second, you were going to tell me what this afternoon was all about."

"Uh, right. Actually, how about lunch tomorrow instead?"

"Instead of talking now?" She frowned, picked up her panties and walked down the hall to her bedroom. "I don't think so, Coop. Tell me what's going on."

"I'm uncomfortable here," he muttered.

"For Pete's sake, get a washcloth for now. This is important." And it was. Though she didn't know how or why, Taryn's instincts screamed that something was way up with him and putting it off wouldn't serve either of them.

"Taryn. Hell, hang on."

She heard the bedsprings creak and his low rumble, then the faint swish of running water. Less than a minute later, the bed again creaked.

"Still there?" he asked.

"Yep. Waiting with bated breath."

"You're fishing, all right."

"Cute. Out with it, Coop." She gentled her tone. "It can't be all that bad, can it?"

"No," he answered immediately. "I don't think it's bad at all. But you might."

Her senses went from screaming to Defcon 5. "I might? Why?"

"It's complicated."

A reluctant smile lifted her lips. "It usually is, Coop. Does it have to do with the Gleasons?" A sudden thought made her cringe. "Oh God, don't tell me they're having another soiree and you want me to attend. No way. Uh-huh and hell no. Sorry, Coop, I won't go through that again."

Not even for you.

A tense silence followed her vehement spew. "Coop?" Taryn gripped the phone tighter. Would he get that upset over her refusal? Surely not. But the way he'd acted earlier in the day, coupled with the screw-up from yesterday.

Yikes. She winced again.

"No, they haven't mentioned anything. But that brings up an interesting question, baby. Why wouldn't you attend if I asked you to?"

Me and my big mouth. "I told you already, Coop, that's not my scene. I don't do well in that atmosphere. It's suffocating."

"Suffocating?"

She heard the doubt in his voice. He didn't understand and that threatened a spark of resentment. "Yes. We've been over this and I'm not going to re-hash it with you now. Drop it. Please," she added as an afterthought.

"For now, but sooner or later we're going to have to discuss this, Taryn."

"We are? Why?" Even as the foolish words left her mouth, she was wishing them back. She knew why. Why was the reason her heart galloped at the sight of him, why her moods teetered on the edge of happy or wistful, depending on how long it'd been since they'd talked. She wasn't ready to discuss why. "Never mind," she blurted out quickly.

But it was too late, he was already going where she didn't want to go. Where she wasn't ready to go. Too serious. Maybe she should break it off now.

The very suggestion made her stomach rebel and her eyes sting with tears.

"We need to talk about the future, baby. Our future."

There it was, plain as pudding out on the table. The future. Their future. Them as a couple. Funny in that all their dates, all their bouts of incredible sex, she'd shied away from the "c" word. Couple.

Her insides quivered, her mind rebelled and her heart sang. Damned if she knew what any of it meant.

Hell, all I need now is a rash.

"Future?"

"Yes, damn it, why is that so scary?"

She cleared her throat, recognizing the rising anger in his voice. "Who said anything about scary?"

"Baby, I know you. I know what you're thinking and feeling right now."

Taryn narrowed her eyes at his confidence. "Yeah? What am I thinking?"

"I'll tell you, but on one condition."

"What's that?" she asked warily.

"Keep our lunch date tomorrow, no matter what."

"Lunch, that's it?"

"Yep."

Taryn mulled it over wondering what the catch was. Despite her roller-coaster emotions and waffling confusion about him, she wanted to know if he could read her as well as he thought he could. Finding no obvious trickery on his part, she sighed, stifling a yawn behind her hand. She giggled as he yawned back at her. "Oops, sorry about that, they're contagious. You're on, shoot."

He inhaled deeply and she pictured him, naked and leaning against his headboard, one hand holding the phone the other rubbing at his neck like he usually did when he was stressed.

Like he usually did…

Taryn's sleepy eyes popped open. Just how well did she know him and could it possibly be reciprocated on his end? Could he know her so intimately despite her efforts?

Was he too close? The logical part of her mind blathered yes, yes, yes, but her heart swore he wasn't close enough.

"Right now you're scared to death. You're wondering what I'm up to and why we can't continue as we have been. And," he hesitated.

"And?" she muttered, mildly annoyed at his perception.

"You're thinking about running."

Chapter Twelve

Taryn sat astride her bike, shades on, helmet clutched tightly in her hands and watched the traffic flow around the busy restaurant. Restless sleep, jittery nerves and Coop's all-too-close observations put her in a foul mood.

You're thinking about running.

With an irritated growl, she rose from the bike, secured her helmet and stomped toward the restaurant. She was not a coward.

Opening the door, she slid her sunglass up onto her hair and looked for Coop, finding him walking toward her, a smile on his face.

"Hey," he murmured as he joined her. Leaning down, he kissed her cheek, his lips lingered, causing a tingle to spread along her spine.

"Hey, yourself." Pulling back, she studied his face. "You look relieved, did you think I wouldn't show?"

He had the grace to look uncomfortable and she chuckled, threading her arm through his. "Relax, Tiger, I said I would come and here I am. I never turn down free food remember? Not to mention the opportunity to have you all to myself for a little bit."

He hesitated, resisting the tugging of her arm. "Uh, about that…"

Those warning bells went off again and she dropped her hand. "What?"

Coop's sigh raked over her nerves and she narrowed her eyes. "Coop?"

He turned her around, his palm flat at the base of her spine and urged her forward. "We're not alone."

They were at the table before she could express her indignation, but she sure as hell hoped her lash-lowered glare pierced him. It would have to do until they were alone.

"Carol and Bill Taylor, may I introduce Taryn Kirkpatrick? The Taylors are some of my clients, Taryn."

Clients. Oh, he was playing dirty, damn him. Taryn mustered a smile and politely shook hands even as Coop seated her. Though neither of the thirty-something-Taylors did anything that spoke of distaste, she felt herself being weighed and measured once more. Carol's welcoming smile couldn't possibly be real and already Bill was checking out her assets.

A split-second of wishing she'd chosen something other than jeans and the blue button-down shirt whipped through her mind before she firmly pushed it aside.

If they had a problem with her appearance, tough crap. Wasn't her fault Coop hadn't warned her. She spared him another speaking glance. The waiter appeared, took her drink order— rum and coke, don't spare the rum— and left her a menu. She thought about hiding behind the elegantly scripted menu until he returned, but reminded herself, again, that she wasn't a coward.

And she might as well get this conversation going on her terms. "Have you been with Coop long?"

Was it her imagination, or did Bill answer her cleavage? "About four years. He's very good."

Irked at his blatant stare, she straightened and waited until he looked up. Running a hand over Coop's suit-clad forearm, she winked at Bill. "Yes, he is."

Carol fell into a sudden coughing fit, covering her mouth with her linen napkin. Coop's arm tensed under her still stroking fingers.

Tough, he set this little party up, let him take the fall. I will not be anyone other than myself.

"Going to be all right there, Mrs. Taylor?" she asked.

"Yes, thank you." The woman's wide-eyed gaze bounced between Coop and Taryn, and smile lifted her lips. "So, are you a client of Coop's as well?"

"Oh no, definitely not." With another slow drop of her lashes, she leaned toward the other woman. "Our relationship is strictly personal."

"Ah, personal, huh?" Bill waggled his brows at Coop. "Lucky man, Malone."

The up-til-now silent Coop pulled his arm

away from Taryn's hand. "Yes, I am." He met her eyes, his filled with determination. "I asked her here today because I wanted her to get to know my clients. Something that is very important to me."

Taryn gritted her teeth, giving him a very forced smile.

Carol nodded. "Oh, we understand completely." She turned to Taryn. "When Bill and I first started dating, I had no idea how important his business was to him. Turned out to be what nearly drove us apart. If it hadn't been for Coop, I doubt..., well anyway, that's all ancient history. Let's just say, I commend you for your interest and willingness."

Taryn sipped at her drink, wondering if the woman was for real. Who spilled personal information like that on a first meeting?

Some of her thoughts must have shown in her face, because Carol pinkened and her eyes dropped. Mouth sour and suddenly feeling like the world's biggest bitch, Taryn set her rum and coke on the table.

She'd screwed up again. When would she learn? When would he?

"I'm sorry, I have to go." Standing up, she avoided looking at Carol again. "Nice to have met you," she mumbled even as she took off.

"Taryn, wait," Coop's strong voice rang out over the hum of the other diners conversation.

She whipped around, angry tears threatening to spill over. "Damn you, Cooper," she whispered fiercely. "This is all your fault. You set me up."

He cupped her shoulders that damn determination still in his eyes and now in the rigid set of his jaw. "No, I didn't set you up. I tried to create an opportunity."

"For what? To make a fool of me? To watch me mess up? Why, Coop? What were you thinking?"

He smoothed his fingers over her cheek. "I was thinking of us."

She wrenched away from him. "Forget it, there is no us. There never will be. I told you I couldn't do this, that I wouldn't. But you didn't listen. Just like every other man, you want to control me."

"That's not—"

"Well guess what, I won't be controlled or manipulated. I am my own person, Coop. A strong woman and if you have problems with that, too bad."

Something in him snapped at her words.

Why wouldn't she take a chance? Frustration fueled by the inability to break through her shell clawed at him. Patience, and hope, gone, he tightened his one-handed grip on her shoulder. Lowering his face and his voice, he captured her angry eyes with his. "A strong woman? You're a coward, just like I said last night. You run at the first sign of commitment, the first hint that something serious is in the works." Letting go, he stepped back. "Fine, leave, Taryn, but don't ever mistake your fear for strength."

He turned on his heel, making his way back to the Taylors, feeling every bit the fool she claimed he'd made of her. His stomach roiled and his soul felt dark, empty and lost.

She ran. He couldn't believe his gamble had paid off so badly.

As he sat down, Carol's hand closed over his fist and he looked at her, seeing her concerned face almost through a haze. "Coop, did I say something wrong?"

"No," he said. "You didn't do anything, Carol. It was just," struggling just to breathe, finding the right words was difficult, "it was just a misunderstanding."

"Oh, Coop, go after her. We'll take care of ourselves."

"Yeah, Coop," Bill chimed in. "Can't take love for granted, you know." He looked fondly at his wife, giving her soft smile.

Coop shrugged, envying their bond. "You can't force it on someone either." Glancing at the door through which Taryn had disappeared, he sighed, heart aching. "Take a chance," he whispered.

Ginger glared at him the second he entered the office after lunch and he gave the stare right back at her.

"What?" he growled, letting his irritation show.

"Coop, how could you?"

"How could I what?"

"Ambush her like that?" Ginger snapped, slamming her palms down on her desk.

He pulled on his tie, loosening the stranglehold. "Ambush? Ginger, it was your idea. And how do you know what happened, anyway?"

She narrowed her eyes at him, lips pinched. "Taryn called me. I didn't tell you to not tell her about the Taylors, you moron."

His heart jerked in his chest. "When? Where is she? What did she say?"

"Nothing good, that's for sure. It's private."

"Dammit, Ginger, this is not a game."

Her face hardened even further. "No, it's not a game. To either of you stubborn idiots, but neither of you will see that."

Coop's nerves felt stretched as tight as a trampoline. For the first time he didn't know which way was up. All he could see was himself falling down a black spiral of loneliness. What was he going to do?

"I did all I could, Ginger. I gave her an opportunity and she threw it back at me. She walked out on me."

"You tricked her, Coop. You were supposed to tell her it was a client meeting, not let her think it was a lover's rendezvous. Why didn't you say anything?"

His cheeks burned. He knew it'd been wrong and that he'd been just as much a coward as he accused Taryn of being. The only logic behind his silence had been his fear that she wouldn't show. Instead, he'd gambled and ended up losing it all anyway. But, in his mind, his slight omission didn't compare to hers. "I tried to, but things got out of hand."

Ginger sighed and came around the desk, putting her arms around him. "I hate to tell you this, boss, but I think you blew it. Permanently."

He stiffened in her embrace. "I didn't blow it, Ginger. The next time you talk to her, remind her that she walked out on me, on us."

Disengaging himself, he stalked to his office and closed the door. Slumping behind his desk, he swiveled to look out the large picture window, wondering why being right felt so wrong.

He had given her the chance to see what the other clients in his business were like. To realize that not all of them, hell hardly any of them, were like the Gleasons. That no one expected her to be the queen of England. But no, she wouldn't even bend enough to try.

He loved her, missed her so much already, his chest ached and his eyes stung. But he couldn't live his life that way. His daring lover preferred to keep her adventurous side confined to the bedroom, but he wanted it all. Wanted her all.

Knowing he wasn't going to get it, hurt like hell.

His phone rang and he slowly turned to look at it, an irrational hope flaring that it might be Taryn. His gaze shot through the glass partition to Ginger's desk, one brow raised, hand poised over the phone. But she shook her head, bottom lip caught between her teeth.

Damn. The buzzing continued and finally, he reached out and lifted the receiver to hear Monica Gleason's honeyed voice oozing from the other end.

"Do you have a moment, Cooper?"

Rubbing at the throbbing behind his temples, he strove for his best professional tone. "Of course, Monica. How may I help you?"

"I was wondering if you were free for dinner tonight?"

Hoping she and Troy had finally made a decision he sat up a bit straighter. "I'm certain something can be arranged. Or you could come in to the office, if you prefer."

"Oh no, dinner is much better for me."

For me. Uh-oh, was she up to her old tricks?

"How about Troy?"

"Oh, well," she cleared her throat and he frowned, wincing when a sharp pain seared his head. He just knew what was coming. Her stutter, however, was uncharacteristic.

"He won't be joining us."

Coop stalled for time, trying to come up with a plausible excuse for not showing after just telling her he could. "Why not?"

"I thought it would be nice for just the two of us to get together and chat. No business, just two friends sitting down for a nice evening of conversation."

Two friends? He'd thought of Monica Gleason as many things over the past few months, but friend wasn't one of them.

"Monica, I appreciate the offer, but I'm afraid I have to refuse."

"Refuse, just like that? No rain check? No sudden remembrance of other plans?" Her voice rose with each question, ending on a strident note. "Cooper?"

Get it together. Even if he didn't have Taryn, he still had his business. Something he knew inside and out. Something that he could control. Again a piercing shaft of pain hit him.

Oh, God, had she been right? Was he trying to control her?

"Yes, just like that." Picking up a pencil, he tapped the eraser up and down on his desk blotter, seeking a way out of this verbal mess. "Look, Monica, I appreciate the offer, really—"

"But you're not going to take me up on it, are you?"

He sensed they were talking about two different things now. "No," he said cautiously. "I'm not."

"Does it have to do with your friend, Miss Kirkpatrick?"

Just the sound of her name seared his raw emotions and he closed his eyes, snapping the pencil in half. "No, it doesn't. It has to do with me and the way I prefer to do business."

"I see." She laughed, a bit brittle, but not as caustic as he would have expected. "In other words, you would never have considered...anything?"

He thought she really did see. Thank God. "No, Monica," he said gently. "I would not have."

"Then I won't take up any more of your time, Cooper."

A sense of rashness grabbed him and he decided to go for broke, to press his advantage while she seemed so amendable. "You and Troy still have not signed the contract, Monica. When can I expect an answer?"

"Hmm, why don't we discuss that another time?"

She recovered quickly, but he was through being a puppet for anyone. "No, that doesn't work for me. I'll transfer you back to Ginger and she can give you an appointment for later this week."

Before she could finish sputtering her refusal, he hit the appropriate buttons and ended the call. Damn, that felt good. Definitely how he should have handled this whole situation from the beginning.

From now on, things were going to go according to his plan, damn the torpedoes and the consequences.

The way Taryn claimed she lived.

Breathing out a disgusted breath, he grabbed a pen, the nearest file and flipped it open, ready to bury himself in his work, something that he'd done all his life. Something that always worked.

Instead of reading the numbers and data on his chart, he saw the hurt and surprise in Taryn's eyes, the fear. Cursing them both, he slammed the file shut and glared at his blotter.

"Coop?" Ginger said quietly from his doorway.

"You get Monica taken care of?"

A smile tipped her lips and her eyes sparkled. "Yep. They'll be in Tuesday."

He nodded, not even relishing the small victory. Seemed hollow.

"Listen, this just came in the mail."

She stepped forward, sliding a heavy vellum envelope across his desk.

He picked it up, reading the return address aloud. "The Bentley Foundation?"

"Open it, Coop."

Slitting open the expensive paper, he pulled out an embossed invitation. "Huh," he said.

Ginger tapped her fingers on his desk. "Huh, what? These guys are huge, Coop. What's it say?"

"I know who they are. Very active in charity organizations. They raise millions every year. I've been invited to one of their gala functions."

"Woohoo!" Ginger danced a little jig. "To heck with the Gleasons, Coop, you have arrived. This is proof positive. When is it?"

Arrived? He didn't know about that, but he did acknowledge the spark of interest he felt. "Next week. The thirteenth."

"Well, write it down, you doofus. Oh, this is excellent news."

Coop didn't even bother glaring at her for the doofus remark, but wrote the party down on his calendar, staring balefully at the date. "Oh, great."

"What now?"

He stood. "It's not just on the thirteenth, it's on Friday the thirteenth."

Ginger giggled. "Good thing you're not superstitious."

"Yeah, guess so. You know what, I'm going out," he told her. "I'll check in later."

Ginger stopped him with a hand on his forearm. "She's not at the opera, boss."

He stilled then looked at her over his shoulder. "I'm not going after her, Ginger. I can't. If she wants me, she has to come to me this time."

The blond nodded, her hair bouncing with the movement. "Yep, I gotcha on that one. Good luck, boss. Can I ask where you're going?"

"Go ahead."

She laughed. "Okay, so?"

Coop managed a slight smile. "I have no idea, just out."

The expression on her face was torn between amusement and worry. "You okay?"

"I'm fine. Just need some fresh air or space or something." He looked toward the couch in his office, seeing Taryn sitting on it, bright smile and laughing eyes as clear as day. "Yeah, I need to get out."

He nodded and left, stabbing the elevator button with a ferocity it didn't deserve. Was this what being in love did to a man? Made him lose sight of everything he'd worked so hard for? Turned him crazier than a loon?

Caused his soul to shred with every thought of her?

The doors parted and he stepped inside, again pushing the glowing number with more force than necessary. "Love sucks," he decided aloud.

"Let me love you," the warm, masculine voice whispered in her ear. Taryn tossed

restlessly, briefly surfacing from sleep, looking bleary-eyed for Coop.

Realizing he wasn't there, Taryn sighed and fell back into the dream.

His hands, strong, firm and knowing, slid along her thighs, sculpting the soft flesh. Hot breath whispered across her belly button and she quivered, reaching down to cup his shoulders.

"Coop, please," she murmured. It seemed she was always begging him, but it felt so right. He felt right.

"Yes, baby, I'll please you. As much as you please me. It's that way when two people love each other."

Again, Taryn groaned, scrambling to wakefulness but only marginally reaching it. "No, damn you," she sighed, eyes fluttering shut again.

The scene shifted. They sat entwined on her couch, watching the fire swirl and pop. Velvet purred contentedly on the rug in front, watching them with deep green eyes.

Coop's arms wrapped around her, pulling her close to his bare chest. Taryn echoed the cat's purr and rubbed against him, inhaling his musky scent. Heavenly, that was the only word that described the feeling of being with him.

Or secure. Comforting. Real.

"I love you, Taryn."

Magical, wonderful words. It seemed she'd waited her whole life for this man, this moment. Tipping her head, she nuzzled his shoulder.

"Baby, did you hear me?"

A loud ribbit sounded and she moved her gaze to Velvet's pillow, only to find her cat had turned into a frog. With another ribbit followed by a meow, she morphed back into a cat.

Shaking her head, Taryn turned on the couch, heedless of the cocoa coverlet falling away, revealing her nakedness. She wanted his eyes on her, enjoyed and reveled in the way his gaze swept her body as though he wanted to devour her. Never in her life had she felt more secure or confident and it was all due to this wonderful, incredible man. "Coop, I love you, too."

Taryn jerked upright in bed, sweat covering her body, heart pounding, fingers over her lips. "No way," she said to Velvet. "No way did I just say that."

The cat blinked at her before sliding into a long, spine-straightening stretch. Taryn gulped, threw back the blanket and jumped up. Shrugging into her robe, she cinched the belt tight, mouth dry, eyes stuck to the bed.

Velvet leapt down, tail upright and headed out the door to the kitchen, meowing loudly. Taryn knew the drill and was grateful to escape the room, leaving the fresh dream behind.

After dumping kitty kibbles into the cat bowl, she downed a long, thirst-quenching drink of orange juice, nerves still jittery.

"No, no, no," she muttered, stomping to the back of the house. Wrenching the cold water tap to full blast, she doffed her robe and stepped in, breath held tight. Teeth clenched, body shaking, she absorbed the chill, hoping it would beat out the wildness caused by her dream.

She snatched her cucumber melon body wash and sea sponge, scrubbing herself pink, but the vigorous motions did nothing but heighten her sensations. It felt like every nerve ending in her body was on red alert.

She sniffled, squeezing her eyes shut. Bad move. His face popped into her vision like a camera flash. Bright, fast and left nothing to the imagination. "Damn you, Cooper Jarod Malone."

Her breath caught on his name and the tears she'd been holding back finally came in a crushing river, mingling with the cold water. Choking on a sob, she squeezed the sponge 'til her fingernails ripped the delicate fabric. Curling her hand into a tight fist, she pounded the tile wall, letting out her frustration, sorrow and rage with every cry, every tear and every hit.

It wasn't fair. She hadn't asked for this. When did their affair become more?

Taryn hiccupped and shut off the water, keeping her eyes tightly closed, trapping the tears. This wasn't doing her any good. Now, not only did her heart hurt, but so did her head.

She needed therapy. Shopping therapy and lots of it. Wrapping herself in a fluffy, Egyptian cotton towel, she padded down the hall and picked up the phone, dialing a familiar number.

Britt answered on the second ring, a husky laugh in her voice.

"This better be good, Kirkpatrick, you're interrupting."

Taryn's throat spasmed and she swallowed the jealousy. "Sorry, Britt," she rasped hoarsely. "I'll talk to you later."

Disconnecting, she sank onto the couch and stared dully at the fireplace, an image of Velvet becoming a frog crystal clear. Shaking her head, she wiped at her still dripping nose. Obviously she was crazier than she thought.

The phone in her hand rang shrilly.

Coop, her mind immediately hoped. Britt's face smiled back at her. "Hello?" she said dully.

"I'll be there in ten minutes."

"No, you don't have to. Stay with your friend, I'll be okay."

"Good grief, spare me the martyr routine, sweetie. I've got a set of ears, waterproof shoulders and a line of credit at the best stores. It sounds like you need all three."

Taryn managed a small smile. "Thanks, Britt."

"Anything for you."

The dial tone buzzed in her ear as Britt hung up. Pulling herself off the couch, Taryn shuffled back to her room, purposely avoiding making eye contact with the bed. Nuts as it was, she felt like Coop was right here with her.

Would she ever get rid of that feeling?

More to the point, did she really want to?

Chapter Thirteen

"So, you going to tell me what happened?" Britt asked as they browsed the racks of a department store.

Taryn held up a silky blue halter. "Like it?"

"Yep, it'll look great on you and answer the question."

She draped the shirt over her forearm and continued digging. "I had the weirdest dream last night."

Britt frowned. "Weird how?"

Feeling somewhat silly, Taryn looked around before answering. "Coop and I were sitting in front of the fire, Velvet was there."

"Uh-huh, and? Oh, look at this." Britt handed her a pair of camel-colored, flat panel slacks that rode low on the hips. "Those would look awesome on you."

Taryn held them against herself. "Thanks. And, while we were sitting there, naked and cuddling, Velvet turned into a frog that ribbited at us. Then back into a cat. Bizarre."

Britt turned, propping one hand on her waist,

a thoughtful look on her face. "Okay," she held up one hand, three fingers extended. "First, the fire represents your spiritual energy and physical passion that are about to be ignited."

"That's all I need right now."

"Second, the cat means you will be lucky in love."

"Fat lot of truth in that. Love sucks the big one."

"Hey, I'm trained in this, trust me. The biggie is the frog."

"Why is the frog big?"

Britt gave her a small, superior smile. "Because, honey, the morphing frog-cat means that something in your own life is transforming for the better. That you are about to become one with someone."

"What a load of hooey," Taryn scoffed. "It was probably the bottle of beer I had before going to bed."

Britt shrugged. "You'll see. So, tell me what happened with him."

Taryn glared at the rack of clothing. "He set me up is what happened."

It still ticked her off.

"He did what? How?"

Snagging a gorgeous, green suede blouse from the round merchandiser, Taryn handed it to Britt. "Here, this is perfect for you. He invited me to lunch. With clients."

"Let me guess, he didn't tell you they would be there?"

"Nope."

"Huh. I wonder why not?"

Slicing a glance at her redheaded friend, Taryn shrugged. "Because he knew I wouldn't go if he did."

Britt frowned. "I must be missing something. Why wouldn't you go? It wasn't that man-hungry one, was it?"

"No, it wasn't her. Someone else." Again, she saw Carol Taylor's face pink with embarrassment. Because of her. "I wouldn't have gone because I've told him that's not my lifestyle anymore."

The sweaters Britt dug through jangled on their hangers as she released them. "Taryn, one business lunch is not a lifestyle."

Stung by the mild criticism, she frowned. "But it's a start. Just like I knew it would be. You should have seen the look they gave me. I was dressed in jeans, for pity's sake."

Britt took Taryn's halter and headed for the cash register. Watching her long-legged stride, she knew her friend was holding something back. It wouldn't be long before she blew her top. Great.

They left the store, bags in hand, and headed for the food court. "Hey, slow down. Or are you trying to lose me?"

Britt immediately adjusted her pace. "I'm surprised by you, Taryn."

That wasn't what she was expecting. "Why?"

They reached the coffee bar, ordered two iced mochas and found an out-of-the-way table. Settling into her chair, Britt sucked long and hard on her drink before answering. "I never took you for a coward."

Taryn nearly spewed her coffee. "Have you been talking to him?"

"Nope. Said the same thing, huh?"

She glared, punching at ice clinging to the sides of her cup with the straw. "Yeah."

"What else did he say? What exactly happened?"

She spilled the whole sorry incident, including the call, but minus the phone sex.

The noise of the shoppers moving through the mall, the whirr from the various fast food places and the slurping of a woman desperate to avoid examining herself sounded around them.

"Well, that's interesting, honey." Britt slid her cup aside, clasped her hands together and stared at her.

A chill raced up Taryn's spine and she knew it had nothing to do with the iced mocha.

"You know I love you, right?" Britt's brow rose, looking for confirmation.

"Yes," Taryn said warily.

"Then listen up, girlfriend, and understand this is for your own good."

"Britt—"

She held up a hand. "No, this is my time. For weeks I've heard you talk about Coop, listened to you rave about your dates, the sex, the way you feel when you're with him. Hell, you even defend him whenever I compare him to your ex."

"He's not," Taryn inserted.

"Shush. No, he's not. He's proven that time and again. But you, Taryn, you are nothing like the woman you say you are. I'm astounded I'm just now seeing it, but it's true."

Taryn leaned forward, tummy rebelling at the words coupled with the sweet coffee treat. "What do you mean, Britt?"

A pair of toddlers, pushed by their harried mom in a double stroller, screamed their way past. Britt waited until they were gone to answer, a pause that made Taryn's stomach clench even more.

"You say you're strong, you live your life the way you want to, but you don't really. You hide from it."

"That's crazy. What do you call the Harley? Having an affair with a man who drove me crazy for weeks before I even knew his name?"

"The Harley is a convenience, an outward symbol to prove something that you don't really believe in. Your relationship with Coop wasn't instigated by you, but you controlled it. Kept him just out of arm's reach because you're afraid."

First Coop, now Britt. She'd never expected this kind of betrayal. God, it hurt. Everything hurt. "You know what, I've got to go." Blindly reaching for her purse and bag, Taryn was stopped by Britt's strong grip.

"No, sit and listen, damn it. You owe me that much. You owe yourself, and Coop, so much more."

Torn between the need to run and the fear of hearing more, Taryn allowed herself to be pulled back down. "Am I really a coward?"

"Yes."

"Ouch."

"Hey, that's what best friends are for. To tell you when you're screwing up royally. And honey, this is a major league mess you've created."

"I tried, Britt." Taryn bit her lip. "I did it once for so long I lost myself. How can I do that again? Aren't I cheating both of us if I become someone I'm not?"

"Has he asked you to?"

"Not yet, but—"

"No buts. He won't. Even if he does, you are a different person now. It's as simple as saying no."

"Saying no to what?"

"To whatever you don't want to do. Face it, you're not the infatuated little idiot in love with the biggest fool this side of the moon. This time you're in love with a real man. One who sees all your qualities, good and bad, and loves you anyway."

"Oh, God," Taryn breathed, clutching at her stomach. "Do you think he loves me?"

Britt rolled her eyes. "Yes. And I notice you don't deny loving him, which makes you an even bigger coward."

Taryn glared. "I'm getting really sick and tired of that damn word."

"Then do something about it. Take a chance. Reach for the brass ring. Go after what you want. It's up to you, Taryn, no one else can do it for you."

Questions and uncertainty filled her. "What if it's too late? How do I figure out how to fit into his world?"

"Be yourself, that's all there is to it. If he truly thought you were a detriment to his career, he wouldn't have asked you to lunch with his clients. Maybe he was trying to show you something. Ever think of that?"

"Uh…"

"Didn't think so." Britt shook her head. "Quit being such a chicken shit and do something about this. Fix it. I'm ready to be your maid of honor, you know. I gotta catch that bouquet."

Taryn tried to laugh, but her stunned brain just wasn't up to it.

Fix it. Simple as saying no. He loves you.

Could he love her?

In an instant, she knew the answer was a resounding yes. He may not have said it, but he'd proven it over and over again. With a horrified gasp, Taryn raised stricken eyes to Britt.

"Oh, no," she moaned.

"What's the matter?" Britt looked panicked.

"Oh, no. Oh, no."

"Honey, I need more syllables to help you." She jumped up and knelt in front of Taryn. "Are you okay? In pain?"

"Yes," Taryn whispered. "Pain. Oh, Britt, he's done it all. I've taken everything and given him absolutely nothing in return."

"What are you talking about?"

Tears dripped down her face and she struggled to control them. "He's done all the changing, taken all the chances while I sit back and act like a spoiled princess."

"Okay, you're definitely a princess, but I'm not following you."

"I keep accusing him of trying to control me, but it's been the other way around. I won't take chances or change myself, but he's done all of that. The Faire, the skydiving, making love outdoors, missed meetings. All of it. I've been so selfish and blind."

Britt nodded. "Now's the time to make it up, Taryn. Take the next step and fix this between you."

"How?"

"I don't know. That's something only you can figure out."

"Great, I suck at that. You know, it's not just in our," she hesitated, savoring the feel of the word now, "our relationship that he called me yellow."

"No? Where else?"

"In my career. He asked me if I would settle for just being the costumer. I was offended, you know, but not because I thought he was putting me down."

"Then why?"

Taryn cleared her throat, looking away. This was something she'd often thought about, but never really planned to pursue. Now, she knew, it was also further proof that both Britt and Coop were right about her and taking chances. "I, uh, I was ticked because he hit a nerve. I didn't get into this business to dress actors in other people's creations. In the beginning, I wanted to be a designer myself."

"What's stopping you, honey?"

She squeezed her eyes shut, not quite ready to take that next step, make the final commitment. "I don't know."

Britt snorted. "Yes, you do. But I think we've damaged your psyche enough for today."

Taryn nodded. "Yeah, I feel like crap."

"Well, you look fabulous, as always." Britt stood. "Come on, let's make tracks back to the store. You need to get something fabulous and I need to hear about this outdoor sex of yours."

Taryn laughed, a real one, filled with relief and wonder. "Forget it, Britt. I'm not talking."

The redhead linked their arms, dragging her back through the mall. "I've got a plastic card full of bribery that says you will be. Let's shop!"

Six hours and the perfect purse later, Taryn unlocked her front door and stepped inside, glad to be home. She set the bags down and headed for the kitchen, intent on pouring herself a tall, fizzy bikini bottom. It was after five, coconut rum and vanilla coke was definitely allowed.

Velvet rubbed against her legs as she fixed her drink and Taryn scooped her up, nuzzling the cat's soft fur. "Know what? I love him."

Velvet's paw batted her cheek gently and stared with unblinking green eyes.

The words sounded right, even in the emptiness of her house. Taryn knew she had to mend things, no matter what, but how?

What steps did a woman in love, but afraid of it, take to reclaim her lover? Sighing, she meandered through the house, drink in one hand, cat in the other. "There's got to be something, Velvet," she murmured, settling onto the couch.

Unfortunately, nothing brilliant came to mind. She needed more help.

Picking up her portable, she dialed Ginger's number, hoping she was at home.

"Hello?"

Her voice sounded slightly breathless and Taryn wondered if she could have possibly interrupted someone's fun twice in one day.

"Ginger? It's Taryn. You have a minute?"

"Taryn, hi. Course I do. Just walked in. You okay?"

"No, not really. I messed up big time."

"Don't take all the blame, Taryn. He's just as much in the wrong. He should have told you about the Taylors."

Taryn nodded. "Good point, but totally moot. I don't care about that, Ginger. I...," she swallowed a smile. "I care about him." That got easier and easier to say. "I need help finding a way to fix this, though. Got any suggestions?"

"I guess that depends."

"On what?"

Ginger sighed. "On just how much you care. What happened really tore him up. I don't want him hurt any further."

"Understandable. But you have to trust me on this one, Ginger. I'm not going to hurt him again, I promise."

"How can you be so sure?"

Taryn smiled again. "I love him. In a forever kind of way."

"Well, hot damn, it's about time you figured that out."

"So, got any suggestions?"

"As a matter of fact, I do." There was a rustle of paper. "Hang on, I wrote it down. Ah, here we go. Next Friday there is a huge charity event being held by a fancy pants type foundation. Coop will be going. Alone."

Taryn's eyes widened. "An event?"

"Yep, black tie, champagne, oodles of money, the whole bit."

"Can't we start with something smaller?" she asked weakly.

"It's up to you, Taryn. Think about it. Got a pen?"

"Yeah," she said. "Go ahead."

Hanging up with Ginger, Taryn looked at the address and time of the party. Black tie formal.

Society.

Velvet, nestled on her lap, kneaded her thighs with comforting pressure and Taryn smiled. Which turned into a huge grin.

"Holy crow, Velvet. Look." She held up a steady hand. "No shakes. Stomach's fine. I can even say it. A charity event replete with bigwigs, socialites and people with agendas. And I'm not even worried."

The cat cocked a green eye. "Okay, a little bit nervous, but none of it matters. All that's important is that Coop will be there."

Velvet purred, crawling up into her arms,

rough little tongue sweeping her chin. Taryn laughed and stood, joy infusing every part of her body. "Ack! What am I going to wear?"

Drink and cat in hand, she strolled to the bedroom. Surely she'd held over at least one decent outfit from those days. Fortunately, elegant ensembles rarely went out of style. "Got any ideas?" she asked Velvet.

The cat leapt from her arms onto the bed, sat and started washing her paw and face.

"Fat lot of help you are," Taryn grumbled.

Velvet paused, blinked and yawned widely before imperiously jumping to the floor. She squeezed through the open closet door and meowed.

She never did that.

"What are you doing in there, cat?" Taryn pulled open the door. She didn't see her anywhere. "Hey, where'd you go?"

Another loud meow and Taryn spotted her, luminous eyes glowing green in the furthest corner of the spacious closet. She sat atop a large, leopard print box that Taryn hadn't thought about in quite some time.

The box that held the reminders of a one-time dream. Before she'd become content. Dropping to her knees, she nudged the cat aside and reached for the lid, fingers trembling.

"You're brilliant, Velvet," she said softly, pulling out sheaves of paper. "This is exactly what I need to do to win him back."

Coop trudged into the office late. "Any messages?" he asked as he'd done every day for the past four.

"No, Coop, I'm sorry." Ginger's sympathetic tone also remained the same.

Taryn hadn't called or stopped by since that disastrous day in the restaurant. Not that he'd really expected her to, but it hurt that she could blithely walk away from something that had been so incredible.

He raked a hand through his hair. "Fine."

"Boss..."

"It's okay, don't worry about it."

"Right, so whatever on that."

He shrugged and continued to his office, slinging his briefcase down on his desk, staring blankly at the papers he'd dislodged.

"Coop."

"What?"

"Coop, look at me. This has to stop."

She sighed and touched his shoulder. "Things will get better, I promise. But I've got to be honest, you look like crap."

He frowned, turning toward her. "Good, I'd hate to feel this bad and have it be my own little secret. And how do you know it'll get better? I hate this."

"I know, Coop. Nothing anyone can say will help either. Only time will heal you. But you've got to focus. Get it back together."

"I am together."

"Ha. Did you even check the mirror before you left this morning?"

He glanced down. "What's wrong with me?"

She huffed. "Your hair is a mess, your tie is crooked and I don't think you even ironed your shirt."

Shifting uncomfortably, he shrugged. "I don't remember."

"Okay, that's it. I've had enough. The Gleasons will be here in two hours. You need to go home, spruce up and get back here ready to work. Otherwise, I'll cancel their appointment."

"The hell you will," he snapped.

"Watch me."

"I'll fire you."

"So what?" She crossed her arms and tapped her foot, a frown deeply etched in her brows. "At least then you'll have to take some sort of action. You gotta admit, boss, it's been pathetic here this week."

Coop balled his hands into fists because she was right. "What am I going to do without her, Ginger?"

Her expression never changed. "It's only been a few days. Give her some more time. You don't know what's going through her mind any more than she knows what's up with you."

Coop squinted at her. "When did you get to be so wise?"

Ginger snorted. "I've always been this way, it's just you and Chris that never thought I was."

He gave her a half-smile as he picked up his briefcase. "Yeah, well, big brother's prerogative, I guess."

"What's your excuse?"

"Watch it or I really will fire you."

She grinned. "Get outta here, boss."

Coop drove slowly home, eyes purposefully averted from the exit to the lake. Then Cuppa Joe's. The cutoff to Taryn's house. Funny how it seemed every mile he drove reminded him of her. Would it ever go away?

Pulling into his driveway, he killed the engine, draped his arms over the steering wheel and listened to the words pouring from the radio. They spoke to him like nothing ever had. The soulful voice crooned about words never spoken, chances never taken. Could this really be the way it was meant to be?

He didn't know. Did Taryn feel the same emptiness? Her silence was hard to judge. Perhaps she was just as lost as he or maybe she'd really just written off their affair as a fun experience and already moved on.

The thought turned his stomach and he fervently hoped Ginger was right and that she only needed time.

Once inside, Coop had to grimace at his appearance. His secretary had nailed it. A few more wrinkles, lose the shoes and he could pass for a bum in an alley.

Shucking his jacket, shirt and tie, Coop found suitable replacements in his closet. As he knotted his now-matching tie, he drew in a deep breath, working on pushing thoughts of Taryn and his irritating despondency aside.

He needed to concentrate on the Gleasons, be ready for their questions and demands. This was it. Whether they signed or not, he would know one way or another where he stood with them today.

At least one thing in his life would be settled.

"Good grief, enough with the woe-is-me crap." He glared at his image in the mirror. "You're not the first guy to get dumped on by love."

For some stupid reason, that made him feel better. Coop left the house, reaching the office in record time.

"Better?" he asked Ginger as he opened the door.

"Indubitably," she said with a wink. "Now, get in there and get ready to make a great deal."

He shook his head and walked to his office. "Sassy."

"You know it," she hollered behind him.

Coop pulled out their file and perused the contract, satisfied with the way the numbers crunched to both of their benefits. Especially after all the changes their attorney demanded. It'd been tough, but this new contract looked good. If only he could get them to see that and sign today.

His phone buzzed. "The Gleasons are here," Ginger's voice said.

He looked up, rising as they entered his office. Shaking hands with Troy, he looked hesitantly at Monica, searching for signs of animosity. To his relief, and surprise, he found none. She offered him a gracious, businesslike, smile and sat down.

"Coop," Troy began, pulling a large manila envelope from his briefcase. "We looked over the figures from the original contract and decided to run with those."

Coop blinked. "The original?"

"Yes," Monica said. "We were unhappy with the way our attorney restructured. The way you presented in the beginning stands to be a much more profitable relationship all the way around."

He struggled to hide his glee. "I agree and I have those documents right here." Shuffling through the newly drafted pages, he pulled the first contract out, skimming over the paragraphs. "You understand that this is a binding agreement? Once all the papers have been signed, we're in it for the long haul?"

"We have complete confidence in you, my boy," Troy assured him. "Should have had this signed and rolling long time ago, but you know how it goes."

Coop avoided looking in Monica's direction. "Yes," he murmured. "That's just the way it happens sometimes."

"Well, give me a pen, Coop. Monica and I are heading down to the coast for the weekend and I want to get on the road."

He handed Troy a pen, leaned back in his chair and waited, unable to believe the ease with which this was happening. But he wasn't about to count his blessings here.

"Cooper, will you be at the Bentley benefit Friday?"

Meeting Monica's gaze, he nodded. "Yes, I plan on attending. You?"

She gave him another smile, this one more relaxed than the last. "Yes, we'll be there. I plan on exhausting Troy on the dance floor."

She took the pen from her husband, initialing beside his scrawling marks. "There we are." Standing, she handed him back his pen, her hand lingering for a fraction on his. "Thanks for everything, Cooper."

No longer getting the man-prowling vibe from her, Coop smiled with genuine pleasure. "Here's to a profitable future for us all."

"Count on it." Troy lumbered to his feet, wrapping his hand around Monica's. "Come on, love, let's get on the road. The sand awaits us."

Bemused, Coop watched them leave. They were barely out the door when Ginger popped into his office.

"Did they sign?"

"Yes."

"Did she try to jump you again?"

"No."

"Well, will miracles never cease?"

Coop looked at the signed contract, a hollow feeling in his gut. Taryn had been a miracle in his life and he wanted her back, no matter what. "I hope not, Ginger, I sure hope not."

Chapter Fourteen

Nearly two weeks and still not a word from Taryn. Coop swirled the ice in his scotch before taking a drink. After the Gleason's had signed, he'd stayed in the office until the cleaning crew came and left and the security guard stopped by. Twice.

He just didn't want to come home to this empty house, filled with memories of Taryn. He even avoided the leather couch, considered getting rid of it.

But he knew he wouldn't.

Another long pull of the scotch found him refilling the glass. The phone rang and he jumped, heart beating Taryn's name in a hope that always turned out to be in vain.

"Hello?"

"Coop? You doing okay?"

His shoulders slumped. "Hey, Ginger. Yeah, I'm fine. What's up?"

"I, uh, was just wondering if you'd heard from Taryn yet?"

He drained his glass and set it on the bar,

flicking off the lights as he headed for bed. "No."

"Damn it."

She sounded seriously ticked on his behalf. "It'll be fine, Ginger. I'm already over her anyway." More false words were never spoken, but he didn't want his secretary to worry about him. And if she knew just how much he did miss Taryn, how often he thought about her and even doodled her name on his desk blotter, she'd worry like a an over-protective mother.

Her disgusted snort sounded in his ear. "Whatever. I really did think that it would be different, Coop. Guess I was wrong."

"Yeah, guess so." He struggled to take a deep breath, wincing at the hitch in his chest. Lack of sleep coupled with too much alcohol was catching up with him and his body took measures to let him know. His doctor assured him that proper rest would help the occasional pains disappear after a while. Other than broken, his heart was in perfect condition.

"What time are you leaving the office tomorrow?"

Coop frowned, sinking onto the bed and removing his shoes. "Normal time, I guess, why?"

"It's the thirteenth."

"Uh-huh, and?" He slid his shirt over his head, barely dislodging the phone.

"The charity gala? Remember? You'll need to leave to get ready."

"Shit."

"Oh, Coop, don't tell me you forgot?"

"Okay, I won't tell you. It's fine, I don't think I'll go anyway."

"What?" Her screech nearly deafened him. "Why on earth not?"

He unbuttoned his jeans and leaned against the headboard. Getting totally naked while on the phone with his best friend's kid sister was creepy, even in his mildly intoxicated state.

"Why should I?" he countered.

"Because you already said you'd go, that's why."

"No one is going to miss me. I'm an amoeba on a flea compared to some of the big names that will be there."

"Boss, I love you, but sometimes you're an idiot!"

Ginger's yell bounced around his ears and he glared at the phone. "Look—"

"No, you look. Those big names are exactly the reason you will be going. The Gleasons were just the tip of the iceberg for you, Coop. These guys will be the *coup de grace* that sets you."

"I don't much feel like hobnobbing, Ginger."

"Too damn bad, Cooper. You're going. Now get some rest." The phone clicked in his ear and he growled as he turned it off and set it on the bedside table.

"Pushy woman." But her concern was gratifying and, he knew, genuine. She really did have his best interests at heart.

Coop slid his jeans over his legs and tossed them to the floor, stretching his frame out on the freshly made bed. With a huge yawn, he settled his forearm over his eyes and hoped the scotch would help him have a dreamless night.

Warm water, scented with some flowery aroma, slid over his body. Coop sniffed, unsure whether he liked the smell or not.

"It's jasmine," Taryn's voice murmured close to his ear. "Very sensual."

Her left hand meandered through the water, breaking the surface to climb up his chest, flicking his nipple.

Sensual. He liked that.

"Where have you been?" he asked, trying to turn to look at her, unable to find her face in the steaming mists of the vast bathtub.

"I've been here. Waiting."

Her hand dipped again, sifting through the hair surrounding his rapidly-growing erection. Lithe fingers danced around it, focusing instead on the tightening sac underneath.

Coop groaned and closed his eyes.

"Waiting for what?" he asked, breathing ragged.

Taryn licked the back of his neck, her wet tongue trailing up to his ear. "For anything. Shh," she whispered, kissing his throat as her fingers finally wrapped around his aching, hardness.

He arched into her slowly pumping hand, his own fingers clasped tight on the rim of the tub. "Taryn," he murmured, fighting the orgasm she was effortlessly inducing.

"Let it come, Coop. For me."

Her hand continued its magic, sliding up and down his shaft, rubbing the ultra-sensitive edge of his circumcised head which sent jolts of uncontrollable pleasure through him. Gritting his teeth, he let the feeling take him over, flow through him until he came, calling her name in a mingled litany of demand, desire and love.

Afterward, he shifted in the still-hot bath, sloshing water to the floor, trying again to find her. "Not yet," she whispered.

"But I want to see you."

"You will. Be patient."

Patience had always been a strong suit of his, but lately and especially when it involved Taryn, he had zilch. "No," he said, whipping around, water flying everywhere. "Now."

She knelt, blond hair piled atop her head in a mass of beautiful curls, silver-blue eyes sparkling with mischievous pleasure, lips incredibly kissable. "Hi," she said.

Letting his gaze drift over her, Coop took in the flushed, pink skin, the heavy swell and teardrop shape of her lovely breasts. Her abdomen contracted, drawing his eyes down to the twinkle of her piercing. It looked different, but before he could figure out why, his attention drifted down to the small circle of carefully manicured pubic hair.

She'd shaped it into a heart this time. He squinted, trying to see through a sudden gust of steam. Something else was in the heart.

He lifted his eyes back to hers, reaching out stroke the downy hair. "What's this?"

She grinned, spreading her thighs apart. "Come down here and get a closer look."

He didn't need to be told again. Lifting her

onto the backsplash of the tub, he slid to his stomach, floating in the water as he looked at her perfectly trimmed art.

Their initials were etched inside it.

Coop grinned up at her, circling the heart with his finger before dipping between her lips, finding her wetness.

She shivered, fingers curling into his hair. "Oh, Coop, it's been too long."

"Yes," he whispered, inching closer, sliding another finger in and licking at her clit.

She jumped, moaning.

"Too long," he said once more before giving his full attention to making her come with as much pleasure and feeling as he'd just done.

Taryn was so responsive to his touch that he didn't have to wait long before she shuddered long and hard, drenching his tongue with her sweetness.

With a very satisfied grin, he rose to his knees, cupped her face and kissed her deeply, pouring into the embrace all his love and passion. Praying she felt it too.

Coop woke slowly, still smiling over the warmth of emotion blanketing him. The dream resonated in exquisite detail in his mind and he clung to it, examined it. What did it mean?

His smiled faded a bit as he climbed out of bed and showered. Lathering his body, he sniffed, making sure his soap hadn't mysteriously changed to some jasmine scent. It hadn't.

Sure, he'd had sex dreams about Taryn. Always had, even before he'd known her name.

Dreams, fantasies, memories. He'd indulged himself in all of those revolving around her at one time or another. A lot.

Coop dressed quickly and headed for the office, cursing himself for being so foolish, for missing a woman who hid from herself and from life. From him.

All talk, no true action.

Damn it.

When was this ache going to go away? When would he quit dreaming about her, thinking about her? He was getting sick and tired of Taryn being the first thought crowding his mind in the morning. The afternoon. The nights.

Especially, the nights. When the last light faded and only starlight remained, when the blackness was almost absolute, those were the worst times. Because then, nothing stood between him and his memories.

"Crap," he bit out, jerking back hard on the parking brake, then slamming his door with enough force to shut it six times over. "Enough is enough."

Ginger was at the coffee maker when he walked in. "Oops, looks like a decaf day. Morning, boss."

On his way to his office Coop grunted, mind whirling with furious precision. He needed a plan, needed to do something to snap himself out of this funk.

"Coop, this is getting ridiculous."

"I know," he replied, setting his briefcase down and booting up his computer. "Don't worry, it'll be over soon."

Ginger's face brightened. "Really?"

"Yes," he clicked on his e-mail, opening his address book. "I'm going on a date."

"What?" Her screech nearly peeled the paint off the walls.

"You heard me. I'm going to find someone to go out with and I'm going to exorcise Taryn from my head. I have to."

"I'm not sure that's the way to go about it, Coop. And how fair is it to your date?"

He frowned. "Good point, but I've got to start somewhere." Looking up at her, he shrugged. "Don't I?"

Ginger chewed her bottom lip, worry in every line of her body. "Why don't you get through this benefit and tomorrow we'll talk, okay? Just you and I, away from the office, friend-style."

Coop mulled the offer over. He could get through one more day, couldn't he? Besides, the thought of asking another woman out turned his stomach.

"Deal."

"Great," she said brightly. "There's the phone."

He chuckled. "Go answer it, that's what I pay you for."

Despite the hectic pace of the day, Coop often found himself relieving the bath dream, getting hard at the most inopportune times and wishing like hell she'd at least call.

When it came time to leave, he was inordinately relieved, glad to be away from the solitude of his thoughts. Hopefully being surrounded by people tonight, being forced to make conversation and pay attention would keep Taryn's memory at bay.

Hopefully. Because he didn't think his heart could take much more.

"I can't do this," Taryn moaned, looking at the imposing façade of the hotel housing the benefit.

"Yes, you can," Britt assured her. "Now get out of my car, we're blocking traffic."

Taryn sighed, gathered up her wrap and small purse then opened the door.

"Honey..." Britt's soft tone stopped her.

"Yeah?"

"You look phenomenal. Now go get your man."

"Thanks, Britt." Taryn grinned and stepped from the car, the nerves in her stomach bouncing around with fervor. She didn't know if Coop would even want to see her, much less forgive her.

The doorman didn't even ask for her invitation, just smiled widely, gaze sliding down over her with obvious approval as he opened the glass door for her.

"Thank you," she murmured, stepping into the lobby. Discreet signage directed her to the ballroom where her destiny lay.

She hoped.

Another smiling man pulled the door for her

and she walked through, breath sharp at the glittering of beautiful people gathered all around. Taryn stilled, cautiously waiting for the panic to rise, for the distaste and disgust to rear. Only this time they didn't.

Relaxing just the slightest bit, Taryn moved among the party goers, exchanging glances and smiles with many of them even as she sought out Coop's tall form.

To her frustration, she couldn't find him.

What if he didn't come?

"Miss Kirkpatrick?"

Taryn tensed, recognizing Monica Gleason's voice. With a slow, precise pivot, she turned to face the older woman. "Good evening, Monica."

To her shock, she was greeted with a wide smile. "Hello, how are you?"

"I'm... I'm fine, thank you." Was she really having a pleasant, inane conversation with Monica Gleason? *Oh, God, she knows. She knows Coop and I are not together and now she's won.*

Taryn closed her eyes, swallowing around the lump in her dry throat.

"Miss Kirkpatrick? Taryn? Is everything okay?" A soft hand touched her forearm and she snapped her eyes open. Monica's hand.

She fought for control. "I think I need to leave."

"But you just arrived, haven't you?"

"Yes, but—"

Monica stepped back, sweeping her form with a slow look. "I must say, you look stunning. Where did you find that incredible gown? I bet Coop can't take his eyes off you." Monica laughed. "Rightly so."

What? Did that comment mean she didn't know? Confused, Taryn smoothed her palm over her waist, taking comfort in the softness of the velour. "I beg your pardon?"

Monica cocked her head and assessed her. "Nothing. So, you must tell me where you found this dress. Who designed it?"

Taryn licked dry lips, heart beating with so much speed, she wondered why it didn't burst. "Well," she cleared her throat. "Actually, I did."

Monica didn't quite gasp, but Taryn figured she hadn't been expecting that. "You did?"

"Yes," she stated with more confidence. "I did."

"Incredible. Turn around, let me see the back." Monica twirled her fingers along with the soft request.

Taryn spun, unable to believe this was happening. Had she stepped into the twilight zone instead of the ballroom?

"Truly, that is one beautiful design, Miss Kirkpatrick."

"Thank you," Taryn said, pride lifting her voice and her shoulders.

"Tell me, do you design for others?"

Taryn hesitated. A dress for herself was one thing, but venturing out into others was a whole different ball of yarn. A scary ball of yarn.

But she'd already decided she wasn't a coward. Her presence here tonight confirmed that.

"Yes, if you're interested in something, I'd

be happy to sit down with you."

Monica beamed. She actually beamed. Weird.

"I have a formal party in a few weeks. Would you be able to get something done in time?"

"Absolutely." Taryn struggled to hide her elation. Monica Gleason requesting her work. Who'd have thought it?

Never me, that's for sure.

"Perfect. I'll get in touch with you sometime next week?"

"Yes, that'll be great."

Taryn watched Monica melt into the crowd of jewel-bedecked women and perfectly tuxedoed men, still trying to wrap her mind around the difference between this party and the last they'd attended together.

They was no comparison, this one rocked.

Monica's comments gave her self-confidence the last boost she needed and Taryn once more searched for Coop in the crowd. Her elation ran as high as her emotions. Nothing could go wrong tonight.

Moving forward, she snagged a glass of champagne from the tray of a passing waiter, her gaze slicing side to side, looking. The cool drink felt great, filling her parched throat and tickling her nose.

She finally found him, back to her, head bent as he listened to a small woman standing close by. Too close.

Taryn frowned, heart dropping. Had he brought a date? Surely not. Ginger would have called and told her.

Wouldn't she?

Yes. Part of her new pact with life was that she had to trust those around her. And right now, that trust propelled her forward. Ginger wouldn't let her come here knowing Coop was with another woman.

"Excuse me," she murmured, tapping him on the shoulder, letting her hand linger.

He stiffened beneath her palm and the woman looked at her, disappointment flitting briefly across her face before she stepped away.

Still Coop didn't turn.

"Are you going to look at me?"

He shook his head.

"Why not?"

Coop shrugged and she rolled her eyes. "Fine." Taryn kept her hand on his shoulder and walked around him until they stood face to face for the first time in two weeks.

Greedily, she studied him, noting the new lines across his brow, the dark circles under his eyes and the downward turn of his mouth.

He looked wonderful.

"Hi," she said softly.

His Adam's apple bobbed before he returned the greeting. "Uh, how have you been?" he rasped.

"Miserable. You?"

Something flared in his green gaze and the lines on his forehead appeared again. "The same."

"Thank God."

That startled a harsh laugh from him. "Don't sound so happy about it."

"I am, though."

"Why?" he asked.

"Well, because it means you've missed me as much as I've missed you."

"Yeah? You sound pretty sure of that."

Taryn ignored the wild flutter in her stomach, the dampness of her palms. She was going to get her man.

"Do you like my dress?"

He blinked, gaze drifting down her form. "It's beautiful."

"Thank you."

"Welcome. What's that go to do with anything?"

She looked around, noting the interested looks they were getting. "Coop, is there someplace we can go and talk?"

"No, Taryn. Whatever you have to say to me, say it here."

Her name coming from his mouth jolted her, making her realize just how important that sound was to her. From him. Only him.

"Okay, if that's what you want."

He glared at her. "It's the least of what I want, but it'll do for now."

Taryn's happiness bubbled on the edge, not quite ready to spill forth. She wasn't totally certain he'd take her back.

"There's something you should know about this dress, Coop."

"Like?"

"I made it."

"You *made* it?"

She nibbled at the corner of her mouth and

nodded. "Designed and made it." With a deep breath, she clasped her hands in front of her. "I also have an appointment next week with Monica to design something for her."

"Monica?" he said in a strangled tone, brows shooting up. "Gleason?"

Taryn giggled, the sound almost shrill in her nervousness. "Uh-huh, I'll explain that later. It's too bizarre."

Coop stepped closer, touching the royal blue velvet at her waist. "So, what does this mean, Taryn?"

"It means you were right, Coop."

"I was? About what?"

Was it her imagination or did he seem to be holding his breath? "About everything. I was a coward, afraid to face my choices and life, afraid to trust." She sucked in another deep lung full of oxygen. "Afraid to love."

He stilled, becoming so motionless he didn't even seem to breathe. "And now?"

Tears pooled in her eyes as all the love and emotion she felt for this amazing man surged forward. "And now I know the truth."

He gripped her bare shoulders, staring down at her intently. "God, Taryn, you're freaking killing me here."

She laughed, pressing her palms against his chest. "I love you, Cooper Malone. Forever."

"You love...forever?"

"Yes," she whispered, frantically searching his face for a clue to his feelings. "Coop," she tugged at him. "This is where you say something back to me."

"Something," he murmured, thumbs circling her shoulder blades, a wicked smile slashing his face.

She hit him. "Cooper!"

His eyes shimmered and he lowered his head. "God, Taryn, I love you. So much."

Coop brushed her mouth with his lips and Taryn thought she'd never felt anything so beautiful, so perfect, so right.

"Really?" she whispered.

"Really." He shook his head. "Baby, you are everything I need." Coop edged backward, searching her face again. "Marry me?"

"Forever." The happiness and tears she'd kept at bay overflowed and Taryn snuggled against him, knowing they'd spend the rest of their lives making each other's dreams come true.

THE END

I would love to hear from you! Drop me an e-mail at jenniferaugust@jenniferaugust.com or write to me at:

1501 South Loop 288
Suite 104, PMB 197
Denton, TX 76205

Connect with me online:
Facebook: http://www.facebook.com/jenniferaugust08
Twitter: http://www.twitter.com/jennifer_august
Website: http://www.jenniferaugust.com

I hope to hear from you!
Happy reading,
Jennifer

Enjoy a sneak peek of
BOUND BY HIS BLOOD, BOOK ONE,
MASTERS OF THE NIGHT
coming in June 2013
from
Jennifer August

Boston, 1888

"Come on, Logan. It'll be a grand night. It's your eighteenth birthday. Time to become a man."

Logan McCallister gave Joseph Kilkairn a sour look. The Scotsman was bound and determined to drag him to a brothel. McCallister wanted to go. He really did. Fear held him back.

If Father finds out where I've gone...

His straight-laced father would have an apoplectic fit if he knew his first born son, the one he'd been meticulously grooming to join the family shipping business, had gone to the seediest part of town to pay for sex.

Darren McCallister did not believe in crossing class lines.

The fire in the hearth crackled and popped. Wood groaned as it shifted into ash. The big house he lived in with his father, younger brother and sister was as empty and personable as an ancient tomb. None of his family had stayed to celebrate his birthday with even a special meal much less gifts or well wishes.

Not that I expected anything different.

His father ran a strict household. Frivolities like presents, celebrations and affections were frowned upon.

McCallister set his jaw as a spurt of rebellion tempted him.

One night out of a lifetime won't matter.

McCallister shifted the perfect knot of his cravat, brushed away non-existent lint from his custom jacket and nodded his head. "All right. I'm in."

Joseph chortled and thumped him on the back. "You're going to love it," he said. His dark blue eyes gleamed. "I was there last week, myself. Had a gorgeous dove named Claudine take care of me. Gor, she was something else."

Excitement thrummed McCallister's veins, easily beating away any lingering fear.

They arrived at Desdemona's Palace an hour later. McCallister climbed from the coach and stared at the elegant house in front of him. A full moon washed over the two-story building and elegant wrought iron railings. Soft golden light flickered in nearly all the windows. A curtain moved on the upper right and he saw the perfect form of a woman outlined against the light. A taller male figure joined her and they disappeared from sight.

McCallister rubbed his hands together, suddenly eager to find and bed a woman with large breasts and a lusty appetite.

Joseph sprinted up the stairs and pulled the discreet gold chain near the door.

"Ready for the most incredible night of your life, McCallister?"

He grinned at his friend. "Absolutely."

The door opened and a tall man with

shoulders wider than the entry looked down at them. Recognition flickered in his black eyes when he looked at Joseph. He stepped back and waved them inside.

"Madam Desdemona will be with you shortly."

He disappeared down the hall and McCallister stood in the entry, looking around and trying to calm his racing heart.

A flight of stairs to their right led to the upper floor where he assumed the actual bedding took place. The entry in which they stood flared out into a long and mostly dark corridor with a closed door at the end.

Sounds from around the house buffeted him. Throaty laughter and deep moans floated from above while from what seemed below, indeed under his feet, he thought he heard someone sobbing.

He frowned. "Do you hear that?"

"Yeah," Joseph said. He rubbed his hands together. "Sounds just like Claudine when she was riding my cock last week."

The far door opened and McCallister straightened, all thought of the peculiar sound dispelled.

Desdemona was beautiful. Tall, raven haired with a lithe, lush body revealed by the diaphanous gown she proudly wore.

The edges flared as she glided toward them. Beneath the robe, her full breasts and wide hips pressed against a white satin gown. McCallister swallowed hard. Her nipples puckered visibly through her dress.

"Good evening, gentlemen." Her throaty contralto wrapped around his cock and held fast. He prayed he didn't disgrace himself.

"Madam Desdemona. You look ravishing as always." Joseph bent over her hand.

McCallister thought his friend overdid it just a bit with the bowed head and near subservient posture but then she was an incredibly beautiful woman. Her eyes were a shade of blue he'd never seen before. They looked as though they were lit from the inside by flashes of lightning. Her mouth was full, lush and ruby red.

"Who have you brought me, Joseph?"

She didn't take her gaze from McCallister and he forced himself not to squirm.

Joseph made the introductions. "I was hoping you would personally see to his entertainment, Madam Desdemona."

Her small smile revealed a set of perfect, white teeth. McCallister found himself captivated by them. He licked his lips.

"I'm sorry, but I don't do that anymore. I'll be happy to set you up with one of our other girls, though."

Joseph leaned forward. "But Madam, it's his eighteenth birthday today." He tossed a wink over his shoulder at McCallister. "And he's a virgin."

"Damn it, Kilkairn," he snapped. Embarrassment engulfed him like a ravenous beast.

The look on the madam's face changed dramatically. Her brows lifted and the lightning flashed in such quick succession McCallister had to look away. He suddenly felt dizzy, breathless, weak.

The madam stepped closer and curled her long fingers around his forearm while nestling her breast against him. "Is this true, Mr. McCallister?"

He didn't want to admit to it, wanted to lie and claim he'd bedded dozens of chits. But he couldn't. Her blue gaze demanded only the truth.

"Yes," he said with a rasp. "I'm a virgin."

Her smile was like a gift and she squeezed his arm before letting go. "Joseph, I will send Claudine to you. Mr. McCallister, come with me."

Joseph hooted and pounded him on the back. "See you soon, you lucky bastard."

McCallister followed Desdemona down the hallway, his gaze glued to the sway of her ass and hips. His hard cock bounced with each step and anticipation made his balls tighten painfully.

She opened the door, stepped through then beckoned to him. "Shut the door, Mr. McCallister and let me take you."

McCallister carefully did as commanded, took a deep breath and turned to face the beautiful whore.

The whimpering woke him. Soft, pathetic sounds of despair bounced inside his head. McCallister frowned and struggled to open his eyes. They were gritty and painful.

Cold, damp cement pressed along his back.

He forced himself to keep his eyes open. The room was mostly dark. A single beam of sunlight streamed from a narrow slit in the wall across from him. It took long seconds for his eyes to adjust to the shadows.

Something cold surrounded his throat. His arms were thrust over his head and manacled to the hard cement wall. Fear exploded in him.

Where am I?

He yanked at his chains and choked as the collar bit into his throat. The stench of piss and putrid water rose from the ground, gagging him. He continued to pull until sweat poured down his temples. His neck, chest and arms burned from the effort.

"It's no use," a weary voice said.

McCallister squinted into the darkness. Three men were chained to the far wall in similar fashion. One man with golden eyes that burned like candles stared back at him. The room was too dim for any other impression but fear again shuddered through him.

"What happened?" he asked.

"Don't know."

A sudden cacophony of noise, voices and movement assaulted McCallister. He groaned against the painful intensity. Just when he thought he would die from the sheer volume, it disappeared.

He fell back to the wall and sucked down a deep rasp of air, shaking and shivering like a newborn colt.

The creak of wood and rusty iron sounded in the shadows. He managed to turn his head enough to see a door open.

A familiar voluptuous figure was outlined in the doorway.

"Good. You're finally awake."